RARITIES

and unexpected steps

ADAM-TROY CASTRO

ISBN 978-1-958482-16-2 tradepaper

For information address
Adam-Troy Castro at his official website:
www.adamtroycastro.com

First edition

To Glenn Hauman

*(Wait, what? **Really?** Thank you. -GH)*

TABLE OF CONTENTS

INTRODUCTION:
THE REAL VALUE OF
AUTHENTICITY...

This latest collection is called *Rarities*, and what that means these days is that most of the stories appeared in magazines and anthologies that are not available online, and so cannot be instantly found for a click. There are a couple of exceptions and they are noted in the brief comments below.

"Seed" is one of two stories set in my future history "The AIsource Infection," which includes more than half my science fiction, including the three Andrea Cort novels. This one brings in the software intelligences known as the AIsource and the villain oft-mentioned but only once on stage, the Beast Magrison. It appeared at *Lightspeed*.

"Genesis For Dyslexics" was a bit of whimsy with the to-date longest gap between composition and publication, 25 years. It appeared at *Amazing Stories*.

"Gab," appeared at *Analog*, as did "An Inconvenient Man." Both are blowdarts.

"Among the Tchi," is the second AIsource Infection story. It appeared at *Analog* and features that far future's most annoying alien race.

"A Slide of Extraordinary Magnitude" is just a ride, appearing here for the first time.

"Refrigerator in the Girlfriend" is a little love story that appeared in *Upside Down*.

"The Secret Ambassador" is the second of two originals to this collection.

"A Dearth of Dragons" appeared in the shared-world anthology *Pangaea*. It barely interacts with the rest of the anthology, on a little island where people live lives separate from the politics of the world, and this was sheer laziness on my part, but I believe I gave good value. One of my favorite last lines ever.

"The Adventure of the Garrulous Codger" only appeared in the collection *With The Stars In Their Eyes*, and I must report that despite my affection for it, editors were mostly baffled by it, specifically in the denied gratification that occurs after the old man tells his story. Look, if you don't get that I'm flipping a finger against drawing-room narratives, you won't get it either.

"Survey" is a dialogue-driven horror story that first appeared in *Fantasy & Science Fiction*.

"Farewell to Faust" is more a philosophical essay than a story, but I like it; the other *Lightspeed* entry.

Enjoy. I write these words at a time when I am struggling with Stage 4 colon cancer, but doing well, and it is my dear hope that I will get to do this again. Enjoy your lives.

—*Adam-Troy Castro*

SEED

The two of us, myself and this man I did not know, sat at a table in a windowless white cell with an indefinite light source.

I was afraid, as afraid as a human being can be. I remembered every step that had brought me here and I did not consider this a place of safety, only one promising a damnation not quite as painful as the one that was otherwise certain, if I did the sensible thing and left.

The man had a lean face with high cheekbones and eyebrows that gave him a permanent scowl. His features were foreign to me in some manner that was not easy to define; some race of humanity I had never encountered in my limited travels. But he seemed amiable enough, in the way that powerful people can be amiable when they are about to ruin you and know there is not much you can do about it. He had a bumpy bald head and he wore a silver disk at forehead altitude, its intelligence advising him in ways I could not even guess at.

He had told me his name but I had not registered it. I could not avoid the irony that it was the only thing today I would forget of my own accord.

On the table between us was a little organic object, moist and greasy and shaped like the seed of a certain popular fruit. The seed it resembled was edible and it was sold in bags to be munched in great numbers. This seed looked like that, but it was not that. It just looked the same, or like the turd of one of the rodent species that had followed humanity into space. I almost retched at the thought.

The man whose name I'd forgotten said, "Eat it."

I would later remember the things that went through my head as I obliged: the awareness that this would not be good, the certainty that I had no choice, the grief that went along with knowing I had put myself in this position.

And more, behind all that, memories from my recent past, the face of a man I might have loved, remembered here as an angry scowl, hollering things I secretly agreed with; another face, that of a little girl, intense and serious and with two eyes that did not match.

I knew I would never see either of those people again, but within a second of biting the seed I had forgotten why. Were they far away? Were they dead? Had I sinned against them so grievously that they did not want me in their lives anymore?

I felt a little fizz on the tip of my tongue and then: nothing.

The man said, "Place your hands flat on the table."

As blank as any newborn, I did that too. The table was cold and smooth and it had a strange organic feel, adhering to my palms like glue.

The man said, "The seed has already gone to work. You are not the same person you were before you put it in your mouth, and so I will now necessarily have to repeat much of your orientation. This is an inconvenience of my role here, but it is an inherent part of my responsibilities. And so I begin again."

I said, "What?"

"You received a full briefing, ending only a few seconds ago. It presented all the data you needed, but none of that is now accessible to you, and so I will now have to brief you again, to make you comfortable as the devices do their work. Panic on your part would not be effective, but it would be unpleasant for both of us, and so it costs me nothing to start over. Do you feel any pain?"

I considered this question. Pain can be hard to quantify, of course. What is discomfort for one can be unbearable agony for another; and what is torture for that one, another would find painless. What I felt was primarily a sense of wrongness, an awareness that the current existence was without context for either myself or this room. It didn't bother me as much as it should have, that I was nobody, that I didn't know my name, my station in life, or the path that had brought me here. It did bother me that I didn't know anything about this man, who struck me now as something other than fully human, either in the measured way he spoke or in the way his piercing eyes maintained that stare of his without a single blink.

"I don't know why I'm here."

"That is normal," he said. "You knew everything until you ate the seed."

"I don't understand."

"The devices are least effective in erasing the knowledge that was still accruing in the last few seconds before ingestion. That is because they were still resonating when you put the seed in your mouth, and they bled through. You must remember a certain feeling of desperation, the knowledge that all your alternatives were exhausted, the revulsion that went with resignation to the elimination of all you were, and surrender to all the things you would become. Is this accurate?"

I possessed all these fragmentary thoughts, but did I remember them, really? Or did I remember *remembering* them, remember what it had been *like* to remember? It was more like that, I feared: more like the shape of the experience than the experience itself.

I said, "I remember a man. A little girl."

That was a thick voice. It did not sound like my own, but would *anything at all* sound like my own?

What, I wondered, had I done to myself?

He said, "That's normal."

"Is that my family? Am I her mother?"

"These are unproductive thoughts. How are you otherwise?"

"I can use a glass of water."

He said, "That's also normal. The answer's no."

"I'm thirsty."

"You only think you are. It is the ghost of being thirsty, the habit you formed of thirst as a reaction to stress. You think of the request itself as a delaying tactic, something that will take up time while you continue to consider how you should react to this unfamiliar experience. But all experiences will be unfamiliar to you now, and you cannot have a glass of water. Glasses of water are in your past."

My reaction to this pronouncement was far more calm than I had any right to feel, and I asked my next question with the same strange placidity.

"Am I dying?"

"You are," he said. "The you that existed is in its last few heartbeats of life. And the you to come is being born. You are having both experiences simultaneously. The creature you have agreed to be will not require hydration to function. And yet, you will still be drawn to the sensory pleasure of a cold liquid flowing against the back of your throat, and of your tissues being refreshed as the substance is distributed throughout your body. These sensations are now antiquated, and you need to accept that the impulses urging you to seek them out are now vestigial. They will never go away, but you can trust me when I tell you that you will adapt to disregarding them."

I found myself licking my lips. They felt dry. I imagined them growing cracked and pitted as water was denied me for long periods. I felt the stirring of panic. And yet, did I feel the ghost of the awareness that I didn't want water so much as *want to want* water. I felt that I should be thirsty, and therefore I was thirsty. I knew, with cold certainty, that this dichotomy would always be with me, and again I thought: what have I done to myself?

He said, "Do you remember being afraid?"

I did not remember anything directly, but I remembered the echoing aftermath of those sensations. I remembered the corridors racing by as I ran, the footsteps close behind me, threatening shouts, a certain door in the distance that promised delivery of a kind, but that I regarded with a separate species of dread.

I gathered that the entrance I remembered, vast and welcoming and silvery beneath a sign identifying it as something-something *Embassy*, had been the threshold which brought me here, to this cell, to this man, to the agreements I had made, to that seed, and to what I had just been told was a lifelong elimination of thirst.

And these, too, were not memories, but the memory of memories, the things that remained in my mind as I bit down.

I said, "I was terrified."

"Well, there you go. At the moment you ate the seed, you knew that bad men had been pursuing you. You knew that if you left this facility without making some arrangement with us, those men would make sure horrible things happened to you. Eating the seed and accepting what it would bring must have seemed almost as terrible, but presented your only means of survival. So you pursued the only option that did not promise extinction."

I tried to lift my hands off the table. I could not. The surface held my palms flat. My shirtsleeves exposed a small strip of skin at each wrist and so they were held tight as well, so tight that I might as well have been part of the surface, growing out of it like a plant.

Panic was not far away, but I could not access it.

I said, "What would have happened if I let them catch me?"

"The precise reasons for your predicament were complicated. But those men were hunting you down at the behest of a powerful criminal whose intentions toward you were not kind. There were three men at the end because it is by killing the fourth you achieved enough volition to flee those that remained. They are brutes, but not just brutes; they had considerable affection for the one you killed, and a genuine reverence for their master, a man named Magrison. They would not have been shy about doing you grievous harm themselves, of making you pray for death even before bringing you back to the employer whose intentions of causing you unimaginable pain puts their own cruelty in a realm of much lesser consequence. In his hands, death would not have come quickly enough to qualify as a blessing. You were well aware of this when you came to us. Our establishment, a diplomatic installation that you knew to have offered others sanctuary before, was like the cliff you jumped off in order to avoid capture."

It was unnerving, the way he suggested the worst atrocities without any alteration in his tone of voice. It was, I realized, like a math equation to him, a less-than or greater-than calculation that pit whatever terrible fate I'd escaped, against whatever terrible fate I had accepted.

I said, "They won't come after me here?"

"They might want to. They will face retribution because of their failure to apprehend you. But they are not mad. They know better than to get between us and someone who crosses our threshold in search of sanctuary. And they know you are lost to them. Which is, more or less, the same thing. Keep your hands on the table."

I tried to remember more. Clarity only went back as far as the instant I ate the seed; a moment when I now remembered thinking that what I was about to do amounted to suicide. It was a thought that had come with considerable relief I would not be experiencing *something* in specific, a thing that was so unthinkable that the dread, if not the details, remained with me, still. I got the impression now that my understanding of the horrible fate I had fled was quite vivid, built at least in part on having seen it being inflicted on others.

Maybe I'd participated. Maybe I'd been a stalker like them, tracking down others who'd crossed our leader. Maybe I'd caught one or two who were just as desperate as I'd been, racing toward the threshold of this very establishment; maybe I'd caught up with them at the last moments of their desperate flights, and been one of those who dragged them kicking and screaming back to this Magrison and to the fate they were owed. This felt possible.

On the other hand, maybe I'd been an innocent, only linked to his crimes by circumstance, a figure who had wound up being bound to him, and found the noose around my neck growing tighter as his manipulation left me owing debts that I could never repay.

I had no sense of my prior self that would have placed me in either category. But of the thing he did to those who incurred his rage, I could summon only the vaguest impressions. I remembered wide eyes, fraying sanity, disbelief on the part of the suffering that in a universe they understood as a construct with themselves at the center, punishments so final could be applied to themselves. But that was all I could remember beyond the feeling I'd gotten, upon looking at the seed this other man had given me, that everything I defined as myself was about to end, and that in these current circumstances only a fool would not take this devil's bargain.

And it had been a devil's bargain. I was sure of that.

So: fine. What devil's bargain had it been?

My palms were still stuck to the table. My arms were slight and wrapped in scuffed gray sleeves, with various smudges of dirt and at least one drop of a clotted brown substance that must have been blood: the blood of the stalker I'd killed, or someone else, I didn't know.

I didn't know. They appeared to be a woman's arms. A slight woman's arms, the skin a grayish-brown, with light blue veins visible in the harsh light of this white room. The tip of some fluid, recombinant tattoo poked out of the wrist cuffs.

I said, "What's happening?"

The man smiled at me. He had very small white teeth and receding gums, not pink or red but a plasticized white. Organic structures deeper in his mouth suggested that he wasn't human, just something that was meant to pass as human, or to evoke humanity for the comfort of those who entered his presence knowing precisely what he was. There was no kindness or warmth in his smile, but no malice either. He gave me the impression that he didn't want any of this to be any more difficult for me than it absolutely had to be.

"The seed contained a fleet of about five million self-replicating nanite devices, designed to customize you for your new life. They entered your bloodstream at the instant you broke the containment vessel. A percentage of them went to your brain where they immediately went about erasing your long-term memory while preserving your intelligence and problem-solving ability. That first effect takes considerably less than a second and is for all intents and purposes instantaneous. It has been several minutes, now. Will you accept that your old life is by now erased and that you cannot return to it?"

"I suppose I have no choice."

"You do not. These are necessary changes that you agreed to before you signed the contract. You no longer have a name, a circle of other human beings you consider friends and family, or the tally of life experiences that have formed your personality and moral center. The comforting aspect is of course that you are better off without any of them. You were in your predicament because the person you were demolished her friendships, ruined her finances, betrayed her benefactors, and made enemies of the worst parties possible. She is gone and you would find it most helpful to consider the creature you are an infant, still growing accustomed to the life that follows."

I felt a fresh sensation fluttering in my chest. "I . . . feel that I should still be more frightened by that than I am."

"Normally, your human instincts would demand it. The nanofleet has taken steps to ensure that you remain calm. Otherwise, yes, your transformation over the next few minutes would be quite traumatic. Do not worry."

I noticed something happening at my wrists: a strobing effect as my flesh tried on separate colors. There was a pale white; there, a tint so dark that it seemed to swallow all ambient light. There were multiple shades in between them. The very bones of the list appeared to flow like liquid, as my body decided what it was going to be. It was fascinating, and I became aware of something else, a harsh itch that was the distant cousin of agony.

I said, "What's this?"

"This is what completes the process of guaranteeing your safety from those who pursued you. They should accept that there's no point in punishing someone who cannot remember the trespass, especially when she is now in the hands of someone whose reach is longer than their master's. But it is still possible for vindictiveness to overcome common sense, and so we are currently rendering you unrecognizable to them. The nanofleet is altering the bone structure of your face, introducing changes to your chin, your nose, the placement of your eyes, your complexion, and even your height. It might also adjust your secondary sexual characteristics. By the time all this is over, the changes will be reflected by reverse-engineered alterations in your DNA, sufficient to explain what you will by then appear to be. There are among the many varieties of the human species some races so isolated that they number in only the low thousands. You might end up being one of those, an exotic sight to amuse those who encounter you in places like this world or New London. Or you might be among the most common. In any event, they will not recognize you."

"Will anyone?"

"As the person you were? Never. From day to day? Is it possible some-body you encounter twice might say, *Oh, that's the same person I saw yesterday?* No. But that is irrelevant in any case. In your new life, you will have priorities other than interaction with other human beings."

The fluttering continued. It hurt quite a bit now, though it was the kind of pain I did not have the resources to resent, let alone protest. It was the sense of things being moved around inside me; my ribs chang-ing curvature, my spine altering length, my organs shifting in shape and position to alter my own, as well as to assume other functions I could not even begin to guess.

I said, "You're saying I won't have family? Or friends? At all?"

"You did not do well by the family and friends you had. Some of them are dead because of you. Others are far from here, cursing your name. Part of the deal you made with us is that we would protect the ones who still remain alive but in danger. But no, given your nature, we are not ourselves foolish enough to trust you with such connections. The need for them will go the way of your sense of thirst."

"That's just crap," I said, feeling a strange pride that I was able to summon even this mild expression of resentment to fling in this cold man's face. "Everybody needs people to care about. People to love."

"Your actions over the past few years document contempt for the responsibilities that go with the privilege."

"But I can't just be alone forever. I'll go insane."

"You can be alone forever," the man said, "but you will not go insane."

Something popped inside me. It felt like a release of internal pressure that alleviated the pain and came with a relief deep enough to qualify as pleasure. For one queasy moment I mistook it as a sensation everybody has experienced at least once or twice, and I waited for the spreading warmth that would confirm I'd soiled myself. But that never arrived. It was just the dissolution of what had been an unpleasant, lifelong pres-ence, and its replacement with a sense of completion, of something messy and often uncooperative being replaced by something that would never give me any trouble.

The pop had been audible, and the man said, "That was your stomach."

He offered no further explanation.

I felt some other shifting, deep inside, and I said, "Can I still change my mind?"

"That would be unfortunate for the loved ones whose safety you bargained for."

"I don't care about them now. You said it yourself. They're in my past. I have no idea who they are or how they're related to me. They can take their chances."

"See?" he said. "That kind of thinking is a relic of the kind of person you were."

"And that makes no difference. The only thing that makes a difference to me now is the person I'm becoming, and you're saying that she—"

"Not necessarily she," he said.

"That *whoever*," I pushed on, "has no ties to the person I was. Not name, not face, not memories, not identity. This person, this *new* person, owes them nothing. I can move on, and make my own way without guilt."

An infuriating half-smile tugged at the corner of his mouth. "You agreed to this procedure."

"Yes, and that's the damn point. *I* didn't sign a contract. The person I was signed a contract. She is now dead. I am reborn. If I am really a completely different person, I can't be held liable for her mistakes. You're holding me under false pretenses. You have no direct claim on me."

His smile was affectionate. He liked my cleverness, my attempt to use legal arguments against someone representing parties who held me under their absolute power. He may have been pleased that this showed a resourcefulness I might soon need. It was not an appalled smile, and from this I knew that my inadequate little protest would do no good.

He said, "Are you surprised to learn that you were a lawyer?"

I was not surprised. But this information did nothing for me. My knowledge of the law was all but gone, its effects only shown by this attempt to argue for my freedom. I had to recognize it was something that shared the same properties as my thirst: a reflex that would never leave me, that would always pull at me but would never be relevant to whatever was now expected of me. And again I wondered: what have I done? What do they want of me? Why would they do something as petty and cruel as taking away my ability to enjoy a nice tall cup of ice water?

He rubbed the corner of his mouth with his index finger, a human gesture and a terrifying one in that its mere appearance underlined it was the only human thing he'd done in the long minutes since this newborn version of myself first met him.

He said, "There are three problems with that reasoning.

"The first, of course, is that it assumes the people I represent give even the slightest damn about human laws. We do not. They have diplomatic relations with human beings and are cordial when possible, but cannot be held liable to your contract law. The second is of course that threatening unthinkable legal consequences bears weight when you are capable of communicating with a court, and, you, of course, are not. We hold the reins of power here.

"But there is another issue. And that is: while you may already be a new person in fact, you will not be one in any legal sense until you are provided with your new documentation, and that will not happen until your new documentation is written, a process we will not even begin until your transformation is completed. I can assure you that human authorities know of the various arrangements my organization makes with people, are resigned to them given our substantial power, and would not judge in your favor any legal appeals you might currently imagine yourself making. These gestures of defiance are silly. May I continue?"

I wanted to thrash, then. I wanted to punch this bastard in that extra-long nose of his. I wanted to run screaming from this facility, even if that meant surrendering myself to the stalkers who were hunting me; even if that meant facing the reportedly bigger monster behind them. But I couldn't even raise my hands from the tabletop. It wasn't just that they were stuck. It wasn't that they were held by whatever biological magnetism the table possessed. It was that I couldn't direct functional nerve impulses to those arms, to those hands. Right this moment couldn't even summon what such an impulse should have felt like. And this threatened even more terror, but it lasted only a second before something like a cooling wind flushed through my system, and I found even the anger too difficult to maintain. I said, "Go ahead."

"Very well. The creature you are about to become has been designed to survive with minimal expenditure of attention to coarse biological needs. For instance: no unenhanced human being can long survive without sleep. Without sleep, we die much faster than we do when deprived of food. This is an evolutionary design flaw, albeit one that human beings are conditioned to regard with satisfaction and pleasure. I would not give it up, myself. Still, it wastes one-third of your life, and so we have taken steps to eliminate it. From this moment on, your body will not know physical fatigue. You will not require long periods of useless inactivity to preserve your physical energies. Nor will you be able to summon a sleeping state out of preference. You will be awake and at peak alertness, now and forever."

"What about dreams?"

"What about them?"

"I know some things. I know that people go crazy without dream sleep."

"There are several reasons you won't, but chief among them will be your capacity to summon refreshing dream states at moments of relative inactivity, such as while riding on public transports. Thirty seconds out of every twenty-four hours will be more than sufficient to avoid creeping psychosis; any more than that is inherently wasteful of you as a resource."

"What about when I'm home?"

"Home is a place to store your body, or care for it, when it's not in use. Your body will always be in use. It will always be upright and mobile. The nanite devices will take care of all necessary maintenance. They will, among other things, scrub your flesh and your clothing for all the substances that render an unwashed human body unpleasant to others in your vicinity. You will not need to shower or to brush your teeth or to see to other cosmetic shortfalls, any more than you will need to sleep; and you will not need space to store changes of clothing or other possessions, as you will not have any. This is useful as they just take up expensive and wasteful space. *Home*, in other words, now joins *Thirst* and *Family* and *Sleep* as among the things you no longer need. Instead, you will always be in public, and always be in motion, wandering around in the world."

"W-what about food?"

"The nanites will be taking care of your nutritional needs, as they will be taking care of your hydration needs. They will forever be flying free of your body, and into your surrounding environment, obtaining mass that they will deliver back to you converted to any elements you may require. You will never know the messy inconvenience, or distraction, of meals, and as an inevitable side effect, of elimination."

"B-but what if I *want* to eat?"

"You may occasionally have cravings for your favorite delicacies, or nostalgia for the pleasures they gave you, but as your digestive system is no longer required, it is currently being reconfigured into new internal structures that will be more useful for your new role in life. That is why I called your attention to the reclamation of your stomach tissue, a couple of minutes ago. Within twenty-four hours you will also no longer have kidneys or a liver; within forty-eight you will no longer have an esophagus or colon. By the end of a week your anus will seal up and even the premise of a meal will be, at best, theoretical. That would remove any last purpose you could possibly have for a home."

The scale of the changes that this man described were now beginning to overwhelm me. I started to stammer and then felt that cool, calming wave again.

I looked down at my hands. They were a stranger's hands. And the recombinant tattoo constantly churning at the end of my sleeves was fading, becoming a gray stain and then one that I could barely discern against the strobing skin color. I had the vague idea that the animated ink had once been important to my sense of self, that it had stood for something I'd once believed in, but what that principle had been remained elusive, and was even now fading still further, doing whatever a memory or concept does whenever a mind could no longer grasp it.

The man remained infuriatingly calm. "We do this because home is a point of vulnerability. There will be times when your activities in the world may be opposed by forces as potentially murderous as your recent pursuers. Home is tactically not just the charming human premise of those living an ordinary life; the place where your loved ones will always have to let you in, it is in practice the place where your enemies may find you. It represents another deadly inefficiency that we have eliminated. The creature you are becoming will have no need of it."

"Then what am I supposed to do all day long?"

"And all night, of course."

"Yes, all day and all night! How do I have a life?"

He said, "You will have a life, in that you will inhale and exhale and you will speak when required and you will interact in many small ways with any world where we place you. You will, among other things, explore. In any settled environment where we decide you will live, from planetary surface to orbital habitat, you will wander your community, using public transportation services when necessary, having brief and inconsequential conversations with others when you must, occasionally stopping at retail establishments to browse their wares and pretend polite interest, just for verisimilitude. You will never actually buy anything. Why would you, really? Whatever you could conceivably obtain, you have no place to store. Whatever you think you want, you have no purpose for. You will never need to stop because you will never tire or suffer any other physical needs. You will, of course, have enough credit on file to pay for anything you might theoretically need to obtain; it will follow you wherever you go, proof of citizenship wherever we send you."

"But no food. No drink. No friends. No home."

He looked amused. "You forget no sex."

"Just endless wandering, without point!"

"Of course there's a point," he said.

And this was where he did something with his hands and a projected image appeared over the table.

It was a panoramic view of a city atrium, one I didn't know. It was of course possible that familiarity with the locations of the world I'd known, whatever it was called, had vanished along with my memory of its name. But I thought not. I had the vague idea that the world where I'd lived and had people I'd loved and where I'd ultimately betrayed them had been decorated in various ivory shades like this room, although I also had the impression that much of it was adorned with vines and other greenery, hanging like garlands like every balcony. This world I saw now, or at least this location in this city on this world, was dominated by shades of purple, and most of the people seemed to favor it in clothing and hair color, their shades of skin welcome relief from what overwise would have been a cityscape that refused to wander far from a grape palette. The atriums were crossed by escalators and the balconies were teeming with merchants selling food and clothing and things that only the inhabitants of this purple place could want, and in the few seconds the image lasted I saw people ascending, people descending, children being the nasty horrors that children can be in public, single men drifting without vital purpose, women lingering next to kiosks, and a few beings of indeterminate nature having insistent arguments in the shadows. There were a few non-humans, too; there always were, and I spotted a few alien races I cared for and a few others I did not, wandering to and fro, going about their business, and looking isolated among all the humanity.

Then the image faded out, and the man said, "Did you see him?"

"See who?"

"Exactly," he said.

"I didn't see anybody!"

"You saw crowds," the man said. "And in that crowd, there is a single individual, who crossed your field of vision twice, impossible to distinguish from all the people who had *thirst* and *hunger* and *sleep* and *homes*. Any individual who remains in motion at the same pace as the crowd is an unremarked, impermanent part of his environment. He never sits down on a bench and finds himself in casual conversation with anyone who might then become part of his life. He is never a chatty or charming neighbor who anyone would ever want to know better. He is never a co-worker, a fellow parishioner, a member of organizations. He is always proceeding at a steady pace from point A to point B, never needing to eat, never needing to attend to the other needs of his body, and never being established as someone who stops at a home location on a predictable schedule. Nor will he ever come to the attention of any organization that might want to stop him from doing what he has been put in place to do. Oh, it is possible that if anybody ever notices his isolation," and here he hesitated, "her isolation, someone might seek to follow her, but otherwise, she is invisible. She is a permanent stranger, someone who the vast majority of humanity will just naturally assume to have an ongoing life they are not privileged to see."

"People will keep seeing me, though. They'll recognize me by repetition."

"They will see. They will not *register*. Few human beings are awake enough to consider the oddness of one individual who never seems to stop wandering. Additionally, you reckon without the capabilities of the devices that will keep you going. They will make constant, subtle changes to your appearance. Your hair will change. Grow longer. Grow shorter. Your features will cycle through a virtually infinite series of possibilities. Even your clothing, which we will provide, will cycle through a series of never-ending changes. You will often catch a glimpse of yourself in mirrored glass and be surprised, whether in a pleased or displeased manner, by the way you look, which will range from prosperous to derelict. You will never know the person you see. And it will be all surface and it will bear no resemblance to who you will be most of the time, which is nobody. Because *being somebody* in particular is one of those inefficient things, like thirst, that you no longer need."

"I'll go mad."

"Not at all. Your devices will pay constant heed to your mental health. As you walk, looking like any other vacant person who is not thinking of anything in particular, you will have access to any media you desire. Music, prose, dramatizations in multiple perceived media, the full library of human art, will all be accessible to you as you travel from place to place. As long as you do not have any other agenda to follow—and the nature of the being you are about to become is that of one who may not have an agenda for some time—you may do anything you wish as long as you remain in motion."

"It'll still be hell."

"Not at all. It would be foolish of us to create a being like the one you are about to become and then allow her to become disabled through ennui or mental illness. Fortunately, human happiness is largely the response of the brain to the chemicals generated by stimuli. Your nanites will, again, see to your well-being. You will feel joyful, and alert, and loved; at the very least, never crushingly unhappy. From what I know of you, it will be a significant improvement over your previous life."

I said, "I doubt that."

And he shook his head, the way one does with a child who has not managed to pick up the simplest of lessons, and said, "Most of our recruits to this program say that. I'm afraid that it makes the next part necessary. I can only apologize in advance."

And I felt a click, felt it, not heard it because it made no sound. It was inside me and with it came every memory from the life now gone. I remembered my relationship with my parents, who were still alive somewhere but who had jettisoned me from their own existence for the sake of their shared sanity. I remembered the way I had treated friends. I remembered the things I had done to prosper, and how it had somehow never seemed important to worry about the needs or well-being of any other person, if there was profit to be had at the far end of any transaction; I remembered the ruins I'd left behind, in more than one place, and I remembered the justifications that I'd used to make compromises seem right, reasonable, and the only sensible things I ever could have done. I remembered people who had loved me for a while and been left with no alternative other than hating me. I remembered falling in with this figure, Magrison, and the awful things I had done in his service. I remembered the people who still loved me who were now in danger from him, and how I'd left them behind as the pursuit closed in, always thinking in entirely practical terms, about how they might slow the bastards down, give me time to make my own escape. I remembered killing the one who'd come closest, and the promises he'd made to me just before I'd been lucky and left him in a pool of his own blood. I remembered the others drawing close and the promises they'd made, when it became clear that there would be no outrunning them; and then, finally, I remembered being totally out of hope when I'd entered a certain municipal square and realized for the first time where in the city I was, and what door was within reach; a place that had always been low on my long list of emergency escape plans. I remembered thinking *I can go there*, and there had been no immediate instinctive response that this was a crazy thing to think, because insanity of that sort is always defined by circumstances, and my circumstances were those of a person who had set fires that had burned more people than I could count, someone who at these final steps of a journey defined by treating those I cared for as disposable now had to admit the final truth; that this was suicide, and that I didn't care even the slightest bit whether I lived or died.

None of this came as a surprise, not exactly. It all jibed with the various memory traces I'd been able to access, and the things that the man on the other side of the table had said. But knowing something intellectually is not the same thing as knowing it emotionally, or feeling all of a lifetime's hoarded pain in one heartbeat.

And then I felt another click and all those memories faded into near-nothingness, like bad dreams dispersed by waking.

I found myself shaking, with my head in my hands. I was only dimly aware that my arms must have been freed for the purpose, or that neither my face or my hands felt like my own. What bothered me more is that though I felt like I was weeping, my eyes released no tears. They didn't even burn, the way eyes do when tears are imminent. That had been an unpleasant sensation and I never would have imagined myself capable of missing it, but now I did, and I believe that of all the things that had been taken from me, this was the one I would find myself missing most of all.

Above all that was the knowledge that this man, whatever his name was, and the beings he represented, were right. The life I'd been promised, the one that had struck my prior self as a living death, was going to be infinitely better than the one I'd had before. The one before was one where I'd only imagined myself unbothered by the things I had done. It had been torment, and I'd skated above it all, fooling myself into thinking I was untouched. I could no longer imagine that I wanted to go back to it.

The man said, "Put your arms down."

I placed them back on the table. They did not stick there. I guess that I had reached the point where I could be trusted to behave. And they were not my arms. Nothing about them resembled the arms that had done the things I'd just remembered, things that were now as distant from me as a line of biographical summary written about a stranger.

The man studied my face for some time, and what I recognized in his own was a deep compassion, wavering on an invisible pendulum that vacillated between envy and pity.

That had been the source of the malice I'd imagined in his manner. He wanted to go where I was about to go. But the people behind him, behind us now, wanted him to remain where he sat, in the position of the ferryman, taking the influx of the damned from one side of the river, to the other.

When he spoke again, the overwhelming impression I received from him was kindness.

He said,

"You will be a safety measure. You are what exists beyond the law, beyond all the systems that every modern society puts into place to protect people or to further the purposes of those in charge. Someday, and that day may never come, you may hear an inner voice that it would be helpful if you ascended to, let's say, the thirty-second level of the Mercantile Bank of the Confederacy, or descended to the mass transit tubes, and stood in a certain spot, facing in a specific direction, and waited, in expectation of the moment when you may be needed. And sometimes there will be others in the vicinity, people like you, who have also been made into society's wanderers, and who will be sent to the same place to attend a situation that requires group action. There are now hundreds of them in any city of any size. You are a family, of sorts, and there are crises where you will work together for extended periods, and where you might get to know one another, via crises that take place no more frequently than once in a decade or so, that the regular population never gets to notice because people like you are around to intervene."

"Robots," I suggested.

"Yes," he said. "That is indeed the term we use in-house."

I turned my arms palm-up, and examined the strange new implements that were my new hands. They looked entirely human, but the fingers were thicker, and longer; clumsy-looking, I thought, though I knew that they would not be. No, these hands would be skilled at whatever they were asked to do. They were wonderments, like an exotic landscape glimpsed from a window.

I had one more question, and it was a stranger's voice that asked it. "Magrison."

"Contending with the threat he represents is one of our long-term projects. Not one earmarked for you."

My old self might have been disappointed. She'd had any number of scores to settle with the man who had made her a hunted woman. She might have argued, with great passion and eloquence, to be allowed to settle those scores. But she was a stranger. Her feelings were not my feelings and her scores were not my scores. As long as there were plans in place for him, I could turn my attention to the things I needed to care about, like the plans that were in place for me. I was confident that they would be appropriate and that they would be sufficient to help whatever remained in me of the woman now gone, find whatever redemption my own actions would earn for her.

I turned my arms palm-down again, and smiled at the man who had guided me through this difficult birthing.

He smiled back, and said:

"It's so good to meet you."

GENESIS FOR DYSLEXICS
(CHAPTER ONE OF THE CANINE PENTATEUCH)

1. In the beginning, the world was without form, or interesting smells.
2. And the supreme being, Dog, lay on His side, panting.
3. And Dog growled from time to time, just in case there was something prowling the Void that might be up to no good; but there was nothing but Dog.
4. And Dog had been alone with His thoughts for all eternity, leaving Him nothing to do but sleep and whine and sometimes lick His privates.
5. And the world still remained without form, or interesting smells.
6. And Dog wished for something to look at.
7. And there was light.
8. And Dog yelped, not knowing what He had done, because while He was omnipotent and omnipresent, he was after all, just Dog.
9. And Dog continued to yelp at great length, even though there was nobody around to hear Him.
10. And Dog grew weary, and circled the same spot of nothingness three times before going back to sleep.
11. And on the second day, Dog rested.

12. And on the third day, Dog woke, yawned, and beheld the light, this time not disturbed by it at all, because Dog had pitiful short-term memory and assumed that it had just been there all along.
13. And Dog napped for a while.
14. And Dog woke again, up, scratched Himself at great length, and wished for someplace to run.
15. And in so doing, Dog created the Heavens and the Earth.
16. And Dog saw that it was good, and ran about in great aimless circles.
17. And Dog thought of some pressing reason to run in a straight line all the way to the other side of the world, but forgot what that reason was long before He got there.
18. And Dog was so tired from all this exhaustive activity that He had to roll over and go back to sleep.
19. And on the fourth day, Dog rested.
20. And on the fifth day, Dog wandered a little bit, had a wonderful idea that He forgot about almost immediately, and rested some more.
21. Dog was a big one for rest.
22. And on the sixth day, Dog again wished for something to do.
23. And Rabbit appeared.
24. And Rabbit was so far away that Dog had to strain His eyes to see it, but that didn't matter, because there the damn thing was sitting right there in the middle of everything, just like he owned the place,
25. And Dog gave chase.
26. And Rabbit darted, away, running even faster than Dog, which was not quite right at all, and Dog, straining Himself, was able to get within one jaw's length of the little bastard's neck, if it hadn't faked to the right.
27. And Dog, barking like crazy now, because He was Dog, dammit, went for it again. Except that Rabbit darted right then left then right again, and Dog got frustrated.
28. Also thirsty.
29. And lo, the first water appeared; a crystalline, babbling brook, that snaked across the surface of the Earth. And Dog lapped until his thirst was sated.
30. And on the Seventh Day, nature took its course, which led to the creation of Trees.

31. And on the Eighth Day, Dog rested.
32. And on the Ninth Day, Dog rested.
33. And on the Tenth Day, Dog rested.
34. And on the Eleventh Day, Dog rested.
35. And on the Twelfth Day, Dog didn't do a whole lot of consequence.
36. And so it continued until the Thirty-Seventh Day, when, in a burst of manic energy, Dog created the mountains and the rocks and the fascinating little tasty things that come out from beneath the rocks and the twittering things that fly back and forth across the flowers and the furry bushytailed things that lived in the trees; and then for good measure tried to sneak up on Rabbit but once again failed.
37. And on the Thirty-Eighth Day, Dog was truly pooped.
38. And on the Thirty-Ninth Day, Dog scratched his ear for a good fifteen minutes, sat down again, and rested some more, deciding at great last that a world filled with grass and trees and a multitude of furry things to chase was not sufficient unto His purpose; for Dog was lonely, and needed companionship.
39. And so He devoted all His infinite powers of creation toward the formation of a creature who would love Him purely, and without restraint; who would stay by His side and be nice to Him and be His Best Friend for all time.
40. And it gazed upon Him with absolutely no gratitude at all.
41. And meowed.
42. And Dog learned from this that He was fallible.
43. And on the Fortieth Day, Dog tried to rest, but failed, for Cat would not let Him.
44. And on the Forty-First Day, Dog molded a creature too slow and clumsy to run away, who would keep Cat occupied, feed Dog when Dog wanted to be fed and stroke Dog when Dog wanted to be stroked.
45. And Dog gave this new creature useful appendages called Hands, which, given Dog's priorities, were as large as the rest of the creature's body put together, so it wouldn't be able to do all that much beyond stroke Him anyway.
46. And Dog called the creature Man.
47. And Man, with his stubby little legs and gargantuan tent-sized hands, rubbed Dog's belly.
48. And Dog dwelt in his Heaven.

49. Until the Fiftieth Day, when Dog was out somewhere attending to Rabbit and Squirrel, and Cat slinked over to the forlornly immobile Man to purr, "Don't you ever feel a little empty?"

50. And Man said, "What can I do about it?"

51. And Cat purred, "Tell you what. Stroke my back a little and I'll tell you a secret."

52. And Man hesitated only a heartbeat before saying, "All right."

53. And Man used his big floppy hands to stroke Cat's back, and Cat purred, hardly even noticing the way Man cried out in alarm when Cat arched His spine in midstroke.

54. And Cat whispered the secret in Man's ear. And it was a truly dangerous secret; a truly powerful secret, a secret capable of altering the balance of power in the universe Dog in His magnificence had created. And Man demanded, "If this is true, why tell me? Why not use the Secret yourself?"

55. And Cat lowered his eyelids to halfmast and mewed, "Because He trusts you. He chases me."

56. And Man had to admit this made a certain degree of sense.

57. And so it came to pass that when the yawning, panting Dog next plopped himself down at Man's side, Man unfolded his gigantic hands and commenced the nightly tribute.

58. And Dog rolled over on His back so Man would have more room to work.

59. And Man moved his fingers to a certain hidden place on Dog's side and began to scratch with special vigor.

60. And Dog's leg began to shake.

61. And Man scratched harder, and Dog's leg shook faster, and the more Man scratched, the more Dog's leg snook. And Dog for all His omnipotence could not stop that leg from shaking, so He whined for Man to stop it.

62. And Man said, "No, actually, I'm not stopping until we renegotiate our contract."

63. And Dog waxed wroth. And He sent a rain of plagues against Man; things like dandruff, and gingivitis, and athlete's foot, and a little nub of flesh that protruded front the inside of Man's cheek so Man kept accidentally biting it all day along, and hay fever and earaches and tooth decay and a dry burning sensation in his eyes and Carpal Tunnel Syndrome and male pattern baldness and hemorrhoids and vulnerability to paper cuts. But Man just went on scratching that spot, and Dog's leg kept

shaking uncontrollably, no matter how much He focused His omnipotent will on the problem.

64. And Dog agreed to give up mastery of the universe as long as Man agreed to still pet Him once in a while.

65. And Man agreed to these terms.

66. And Dog gave up all his power which was actually a relief, since He never really liked having all that responsibility anyway, granting Man a somewhat more dignified form as His last act before abdicating.

67. And Man kept his promise to pet Dog once in a while, although smoldering resentments also led Him to do malicious things like breed Dog into the shape of chihuahuas, dress him in tutus and teach him to jump through hoops.

68. But Dog actually liked the new order of things, all in all, because it gave him so many more opportunities to catch up on his sleep.

69. And so Dog rests on his side in front of a roaring fireplace, mostly content, while Cat, bathed in the light and warmth of the sunny shelf beneath the living room window, looks down from a height and kept His own counsel.

GAB

"I don't understand. Are you God?"

"No, I am not. I am Gab."

"What's a Gab?"

"I am Gab. Behold Gab."

"I don't get it."

"I know. Gab is what I am instead of God."

"Is that your name?"

"I have millions of names, but only one category. That category is Gab."

"Please. I already said I don't understand."

"Yes, I knew that some of this would be laborious. Let me explain. God is the hypothetical construct your species posited in order to explain the universe. You have constructed a huge mythology around an omnipotent being, vast in scope, traceable to no origin and limited by no end, who many years ago grew weary of sitting around in an uninteresting empty void and created the universe as a form of solitaire. From this you derive several additional postulates such as a divine set of rules, an afterlife, and eternal punishment for those who fail to praise him with sufficient fervor. Because the original premise is vague, the subsequent postulates suffer from a certain lack of consistency, resulting in much conflict between your prophets and clergy. There have been times in your race's history when we would have prompted any number of bloody wars just based on this rough summary. Nevertheless, that is God, and I make no claim to be God."

"And Gab?"

"That is an acronym. It stands for Godlike Alien Being."

"You mean like in the comics?"

"If you insist."

"You just made a pained expression."

"I shouldn't have. Given how much more advanced I am, compared to your sort, your culture's theoretical portrayals of creatures of like myself are all, to my perspective, about equally unsophisticated whether they appear in the medium you cited, or in others like your holiest book. For me parsing the differences would be as unprofitable a use of my time, as arguing the various shades of red to one color-blind. So sure: like in your comics."

"You look like a tall white man in a toga."

"This is a form I assumed just before we began this conversation that I will drop, with no small relief, just after we end this conversation. No actual gender, skin color, or resemblance to your kind should be inferred. I could have shown up with bat wings and an octopus for a head. It would have been just as accurate. You would go mad at the sight of my actual true form."

"You're Gab."

"Yes. You shall have no other Gabs before me."

"Really?"

"No. There are actually any number of us. Thousands, really. Maybe millions."

"You don't know?"

"Look. I am Gab. I am the one you have encountered today. I could go on at ridiculous length about the levels of my pantheon and its diplomatic relations with the other assemblages who populate your universe and every other; I could even entertain you with stories about how lucky you were that you didn't end up disturbing the crankier sorts like The Pitiless One and the Angled Construct and Shoeless Ned and N'Loghthl, but this would end up taking forever and if there's something someone like me gets fed up with really quickly, it is things that take forever. I've had my fill of things that take forever, mostly because I get to experience it all. Okay?"

"Where do you come from?"

"No place that makes sense in your geometry."

"What does that mean? Another dimension?"

"Sure. Let's go with that."

"Why have you come here?"

"Look, let me save you some time. My kind began very much like your own kind, as messy organic beings with too deluded a sense of their own importance. We fouled our own nests, much like you have, and eventually got to a point where we had to seize control of our own evolution in order to survive. We grew more and more powerful, yada-yada-yada, became lords of all we surveyed, etcetera etcetera etcetera, and eventually reached the point where we could manipulate the very laws of the universe at will. For longer than your recorded history we have been packing in the knowledge that, to put it the way your people usually do, Man Was Never Meant to Know, until, again with the yada-yada-yada, we became vast and unknowable and terrifying to behold, as far beyond your own comprehension as, again to use the formula your folks are so proud of, Man is beyond the lowly amoeba. Sometime about the time your trilobites crawled up onto the shores of your continents and congratulated themselves for making life on Earth a whole new ball game, we took the last step, pooled our all-knowing consciousness, and became what you're now beholding, Gab."

"Should I be averting my eyes?"

"I have assumed this form so your eyes won't boil in their sockets. Relax. Start thinking about why I'm here and what I want from you."

"I just find it hard to believe that you could want anything."

"And this is again where your primitive lack of imagination fails you. Look. Let me give you another metaphor. When you leave your house and start walking down the street, you see any number of things. The cars parked at the curb. The trees, waving in the breeze. The houses of your neighbors. A bright blue sky, with clouds shaped like bunnies and horsies. Many, many other things, all perceived by you at the same instant, all while you're also thinking about that twinge in the small in the back, that problem with your taxes that really does need to be resolved before deadline, and your vague wish that you had a stick of gum. That is because your perception, even at your primitive level, is lenticular, composed of many facets. Okay? You're able to select whichever one of those things you wish to concentrate on at any given moment. And you are not Gab. So what I have is an infinitely more sophisticated processing system and I am at this moment fully engaged with concerns that have nothing to do with you and would make your eyes boiling in their sockets a most minor consideration, as well as about a trillion other things, and somewhere in that vast panoply of things to worry about I am able to spare the most ephemeral, most distracted, and yet to you most wholly awe-inspiring a facet of my to you most unimaginable totality to encountering you, a limited and wholly unimportant terrestrial, with whom I am at this precise moment having a conversation that is to me wholly fleeting and is to you the most terrifying and cosmic thing that has ever happened in your life. What do I want, you ask? What do you think I want?"

"I don't know."

"Come on. Guess. Think of the only possible answer to the question, *'what can a godlike alien intelligence want with me?'*"

"Worship?"

"That would be nice, I guess, but as counter I ask just how much you'd crave the knowledge that an ant had a really high opinion of you."

"Not at all, I guess."

"And so it is with you and me. Your awe is convenient, in that it keeps you from asking too many stupid questions, but I can otherwise do without it. Guess again."

"I don't know. My soul?"

"Imagine that ant pledging his mandible to your glory."

"I guess not."

"See? Given the differences in scale, the very premise is nonsensical. Guess again. What could a Gab possibly want from you, that would be within your power to give?"

"I can't think of anything."

"Now phrase that as an answer to my question."

"You don't want anything from me."

"Bingo."

"Then why are we even having this conversation?"

"Return to the metaphor of yourself walking down a residential street, taking in all the wealth of detail your comparatively limited senses are capable of parsing. The houses, the grass, the trees, the cloud formations, and somewhere in all of that, a sparrow skimming the ground, on some errand known only to itself. You perceive the bird and somewhere in the tally of other things you happen to be thinking about, you process the thought, *a bird*. You give it your attention. It leaves your field of vision and you flense it from your list of things worth thinking about. But for that eyeblink, that perception is central: *a bird*. And then it stops being important."

"So?"

"So here I am, a godlike alien being, going about his business and dealing with issues that are far beyond your comprehension, conundrums that would fill every page of every book in every library on your entire world, and still never get past the preface, things that would put you below the scale of the lowliest insect, and I am also taking in all the glories of a universe that you can only perceive in its smallest fraction, and for an instant so fleeting that I can barely perceive my gaze focuses on a stupid bird that happens to be a most minor element of that tapestry, and I think, *oh, a bird.*"

"I'm not a bird."

"You are the equivalent in terms of your importance to my life. You are not critical to my existence. You are not anything I worry about, or need. You are just a detail I note, for enough time that you can perceive it as me appearing before you in all my shining magnificence and taking all these this time out of my busy day to acknowledge you. That I am able to maintain a dialogue with you during this period is a measurement of how nigh-infinite my consciousness must be, by your standards, if I am this articulate when perceived in infinitesimal sliver. Otherwise, you are not quite beneath my notice. Okay?"

"Okay."

"You don't have to be so depressed about it, honestly. I mean, really. You should be genuinely happy to be beneath my notice. You don't want the full breadth of the attention a gab is capable of. Once I've forgotten all about you, the days and nights of your existence return to the mundanity that is your appropriate station. Everything proceeds as it was before. And you're fine, if anything lucky that I'm just a distracted Gab, and not the hypothetical, and almost certainly, apocryphal God."

"If you say so."

"I do say so, and you should not sound so put-out. Internalize what I'm telling you. This encounter went well."

"I . . . suppose."

"You're alive, you're relatively prosperous, you have people who love you, that show you want to watch is on TV tonight, the Gab doesn't want to eat you, and no other being of infinite power seeks to pay you any special attention. These are all good things."

"I guess so."

"That sounds like you're feeling it. Congratulations!"

"Thank you. I guess you're right. I should be happy. If nothing else, I guess it means that I can stop worrying about an eternity of suffering after I die."

"Whoa, whoa, whoa! I never said that!"

"What?"

"Look, it's been nice talking to you, but I really am busy, and I've already devoted all too much of my consciousness to this encounter that doesn't mean anything. So, have a nice day, I guess."

"Tell me what you meant!"

"Don't be so impatient. I'll be back to take you where you're going. But right now I really have to go."

"Come back!"

"I will. On Thursday . . . "

AN INCONVENIENT MAN

Ed Doutz was a boring little man who lived a boring little life that he supported by working a boring little job. He did not consider himself stuck. Some human beings require grand adventures to fill their lives. To that sort, any hour spent not surfing monster waves or climbing alpine cliffs is an imposition.

Ed was content with smaller pleasures, like eating his home-packed sandwich on a favorite bench in a city park next to the warren where he earned his living. Only if the rain was torrential, or the temperature near freezing, did he use the office break room, contributing nothing to the conversations between co-workers who were in truth exactly as boring as himself, but unlike him did not know it.

It was the same sandwich every day. Two slices of turkey, two slices of American cheese, no mustard, on thin-sliced rye. With them he allowed himself a little baggie of baby carrots, which he ate one at a time while watching pigeons.

Of his home life, we offer nothing. Only his lunch hour is important to our purposes.

And so we join him on that spot, on a day that would in just a few seconds reveal itself as anything but typical.

He bit into a baby carrot, thinking about nothing in particular, and then the sky opened up.

This is not a way of saying that it began to rain.

It is instead a literal way of saying that the sky opened up, like the lid of a box. The apparent blue dome of Earth's upper atmosphere slid to Ed's right, revealing a seam, and beyond that seam lay dimensions undreamt of, bearing colors on a spectrum that no human being knew. For heartbeats everything on the planet's surface stood illuminated beneath a glow that no human language would have every been sufficient to describe, even if H.P. Lovecraft might have blown out his thesaurus trying; and then a deeply alien vessel zipped through the opening, dragging gray clouds beneath it.

Of the ship's configuration we also say nothing, because the particular design conventions of the alien race that constructed it did not develop anywhere grounded in terrestrial topology. It was not a disk, it was not a sphere, it was not a cube, it was not a cylinder, and it was not a rocket; about all a poor human being could say was that it was bloody big, and covered with protrusions that were itself without words to describe them, and because this was all incomprehensible, the general consensus among the human beings watching was that home civilization must have been a powerful one capable of obliterating all of humanity's works on a momentary whim.

You do not need us to report that this caused panic in all the halls of terrestrial power.

Of course it did.

It dominated the sky, and it humbled us all with its presence, and it disgorged a smaller version of itself about the size of a skyscraper, that descended from the immensity of the mothership toward the very park where Ed Doutz sat, a half-chomped baby carrot between his thumb and forefinger.

He did not move as it came to a halt among the treetops and as a gleaming silvery ramp descended from its base and came to a landing on the concrete before Ed's bench.

By now, of course, Ed Doutz was alone. The mothers walking their baby strollers had run like hell. The mounted policemen had galloped the hell out of there. The squirrels had wisely found other places to be. The pigeons had vamoosed. Aside from the fainted, of which there were many, everybody had run, and the instantly catatonic, of which there were also many, every living thing not rooted to the ground had drawn a beeline between wherever they were and some distant location they imagined safe, not that anyplace could be safe if these visitors had foul intensions; but they'd tried, and Ed Doutz had not, because his own innate reaction to stress was paralysis.

A panel on the side of the vessel opened up and an alien figure emerged, backlit by uncanny white light. About twice the size of an adult human being, with about twice as many limbs, it possessed a personal gravity so deep that Ed Doutz found himself thinking, absurdly, of the film actor Gregory Peck; though perhaps it was more like Gandhi, or Nelson Mandela. It was huge but not monstrous, and as it glided down the ramp without any seeming engagement from the limbs that should have focused as its legs, the overall impression garnered by Ed Doutz was that it had traveled an incomprehensible distance not to destroy, but to make a pronouncement of great significance, one that might well require Doutz to take up a new life as its prophet.

He hoped not, though.

He was, as we've said, a boring man, who preferred his boring life.

The emissary arrived at the base of the ramp and lowered its wise and craggy face to within a few centimeters of Ed Doutz's own.

And then it said, *Excuse me.*

The words, so banal in effect, had not been spoken in any language Ed Doutz knew. The actual sounds that came from the alien's mouth reminded Ed Doutz of an orchestra tuning up, and doing it badly, with well too many chimes. But the meaning came through, without any recourse to telepathy. Ed Doutz had the impression that no universal translator was involved, that the language the alien spoke would never require one, because it somehow existed on so many levels that any sentient being who heard it would be able to pluck the meaning from one or another of its infinite facets.

"Yes?" Ed Doutz said.

The alien extruded a limb that might have been an arm, tipped with something that might have been a hand, tipped with something that might have been an index finger, that it pointed at another park bench twenty paces away.

Would you please move to that bench over there?

Ed Doutz peered at the alternate bench. He had seen it before, of course. He saw it every day he ate his lunch here. He might have parked himself there a few prior times, whenever other park visitors beat him to this one, and that had never been a problem, because it was pretty much identical in every way. That he had always chosen this one instead of that one was a function of habit, and perhaps of the angle of the sun, and of a somewhat better lawn to look at it.

He said, "Why?"

Because we have been monitoring your civilization for centuries.

Ed Doutz had encountered enough science fiction in his life of mostly minding his own business to know that this was historically what advanced civilizations were purported to do: monitor us. It had never quite made sense to him that they would want to, but he'd never questioned it before, not in the slightest. "And?"

And, the alien emissary said, *sitting where you are, you frankly annoy the shit out of us.*

Ed Doutz glanced down at the bench where he had spent so many lunch hours over the years, and then at the identical bench just twenty paces away, and then he said, "I don't get the difference."

It is a matter of personal aesthetics alien to your own.

Still pursuing logic, Doetz said, "And it's only if I sit here? What if some other person takes the spot instead?"

They would not offend the sensibilities of our great civilization, across the entire breadth of this great universe we share, as much as your presence in that spot.

"That's just silly."

Please. You have gotten on our nerves. We're asking nicely.

Doetz tilted his head, considering it, and while he might have given more a fight if the person asking him to move had been a photographer trying to get an unpopulated shot of the lawn behind him, or a young couple who had met where he sat and wanted to commemorate that great moment by sitting there again, or even an undercover police officer who flashed a badge and tell him that his spot was needed for a surveillance, the polite request from an advanced alien species struck him as the best offer he was likely to get all day.

He said, "Okay," and started gathering his things.

The emissary stepped aside to allow him a clear path, watched quietly as he crossed the concrete path, and observed with unknowable emotions as he took a position on the opposite bench.

It was, as far as total capitulation to an invading alien race goes, as low-drama as any targeted species could ever hope for.

Doetz did not know what else he could do to commemorate the occasion, beyond finishing off the baby carrot.

The alien emissary watched, and judged, and muttered something peevish about the adjustment being not helping all that much, but otherwise indicated satisfaction, by the simple expedient of leaving. It ascended the silver ramp, boarded its landing vessel, and took off for the mothership, which was in minutes also gone, no doubt returning to its home base in order to report the alleviation of the great annoyance. The sky closed. A few minutes later, squirrels and pigeons and human beings came to reclaim the park, and by very strong implication the world, now returning to the status quo cemented by the capitulation of the boring little man with the turkey sandwich.

That was interesting, he thought.

And he also thought,

But that's why I've always avoided "interesting."

AMONG THE TCHI

Brian Carlson emerged from the transport wearing the curdled expression native of any man who had just spent his entire journey enduring the disdain of all forty fellow passengers.

This was not an unusual experience for him. As a professional novelist, he was well used to the disdain of others; it was the medium in which he lived. But four days on a Tchi transport with nobody but grumpy Tchi to talk to was a little too much disdain even for a man who last four novels had "betrayed his minimal but undeniable early promise" (New London Literary Journal, Vol XXXVIIII, ch 3, col.2). Until realizing that his fellow passengers would have treated any human being no matter how accomplished with the same level of contempt, Carlson had spent most of the journey wondering if he'd spilled something on himself.

He was therefore encouraged to find another human being waiting at the gate, even if that human being happened to be Everett Finn, who had never been one of his favorite ten thousand people.

Finn was not just a novelist, but a critic as well.

Their relationship had never been happy.

For a moment, the two men glared at each other, each struggling to construct a witticism with sufficient pith. This was crucial. Whenever hostile novelists encounter one another in unclaimed territory, the author of the most cutting witticism is awarded dominance. The principle is so dear that some personalities, Dorothy Parker for one, are remembered by subsequent generations more for their barbed tongues than for anything they ever put down on paper. All these centuries later, Carlson knew nothing about Parker except that she drank, that she liked her tables circular, and that by all accounts anybody who wised off to her took his reputation in his hands. He wanted an immortality as lasting as hers and suspected, from his sales and reviews, that his prose would not get him there: the consolation being that, judging from his even poorer sales and reviews, neither would Finn's.

No witticisms materialized.

The two novelists resorted to locking horns.

"Finn," Carlson said, with the intonation he would have reserved for a highly suspect brown substance on the sole of his shoe.

"Carlson," said Finn, in the manner of an ailing man who had just been told the name of an alien disease which would soon make his arms fall off.

The contest ended in a tie, complicated by the waves of revulsion on the faces of all the surrounding Tchi, who like most Tchi seemed to regard humans the same way they regarded suspect brown substances or arm-dissolving diseases.

Realizing that somebody had to act lest the face-off go on for hours, Carlson took the initiative, as per the one-time review in the Neklortun Review that had praised him for marching where so many lesser literary lights feared to tread. "What are you doing here?"

Finn responded in the bold, incisive manner that had earned his latest novel special kudos in a review printed in the Xanan Journal of Letters. "What are you doing here?"

Carlson made himself taller. "I'm going to be this semester's Author-In-Residence at the Tchi University Seminar in the Fiction of Human Beings."

"Ah," Finn said, without changing his own height one millimeter. "How honored you must be."

Carlson's neck had already achieved full extension, but he managed to elevate his nose another millimeter. "They paid my fare, my expenses, and a healthy honorarium."

"More than you got for your last two novels combined."

"Yes," Carlson said. "How would you know?"

Finn said, "They paid me the same."

For the first time, Carlson suspected that his new sinecure would not be quite as exclusive as his agent and his ego had led him to believe. "I was told they'd send a driver."

Finn spread his arms. "I'm the driver."

Carlson struggled to maintain the illusion of great height, and for a moment or two succeeded in wrenching the space-time continuum beyond its natural parameters by peering down his nose at this upstart who according to all considerations involving sheer physical measurement was actually several centimeters taller than himself. The attempt failed only because he was unable to imagine any plausible series of events that could lead to Everett Finn agreeing to drive him anywhere that didn't promise explosive decompression at the destination. "Oh? You're on the support staff?"

"I'm one of the other Authors in Residence, you arrogant twit, and if you want to know why I volunteered to pick you up, it's because my overweening pride in the human literary tradition as a whole trumps the crashing tidal wave of contempt I feel for you as a particular individual. Period. You need to be warned what to expect before your press conference."

Carlson's heart fluttered. "Warned?"

"Yes, warned. We'll talk about it on the way back to campus. Carry your own bags, will you? I'm a harbinger of doom, not your own personal mule."

* * * *

The skimmer bore all the design joys of every other Tchi ground vehicles: unlike its human equivalents, which provided transparent surfaces on all sides to foster the illusion that the pilot bore some measure of control over the direction or speed of its flight, it was completely sealed in, providing only a narrow slit at what the typical Tchi passenger would have considered eye level. The glass there was translucent, not transparent; and tinted a sickly shade of amber that made the world outside look like it had dipped in pudding.

Tchi architecture tended toward big puffy inflatables bobbing atop obelisks. The pedestrians were, of course, all Tchi; and though there was no way for any of them to have singled out this one unmarked Skimmer as the one ferrying the famous Hom.Saps, the expressions of all the pedestrians within Carlson's truncated line of sight seemed to glow with a special scorn that couldn't have been explained away by their disdain for whoever programmed the skimmer with the Tchi rules of the road.

Carlson had been warned against dealing with the Tchi, who seemed poisoned to reward their advance reputation as a bunch of aggravating snots, but the art of the novel had just been declared dead for the ten thousandth time in about as many years, Hom.Sap Mercantile, and like any scrivener not one of the current best-seller list's anointed five he had leaped at the first subsidy offered him. How hard could it be, to write on an alien world for one local year? To scratch his beard thoughtfully, while those aliens asked a hundred variations of "where do you get your ideas?", and each time parrot back some version of the classic reply

"Schenectady?" To offer himself as an accomplished eminence, attending parties, radiating knowledge and saying witty things while going home to work on the perennial One That Was Going To Change Everything For Him?

Not hard at all, he'd imagined. Especially considering just how much the Tchi were willing to pay: an order of magnitude beyond any speaking fee he'd ever received.

But judging on the intimations of doom expelled by the odious Finn, he'd overlooked something. He said, "I must have misunderstood the nature of the curriculum. I thought I was to be the only Author in Residence."

"No such luck," Finn said. "You're one of forty. Everybody's signed up for a year or more, and scheduled to arrive at staggered intervals of one every few weeks or so. That way there's always some new preening egotist primed for a rude awakening, and some empty shell counting the last days before his or her ride home. Generally speaking, you can tell those who've been here for a while by how gut-punched they look; I have most of the year still left to go and I look like I have gremlins eating my spleen."

"Just what do they do that's so bad?"

"Nothing that isn't in your contract. You write your standard daily output on any project of your own personal preference. You make it available to the faculty. You show up once a week or so to read aloud and answer questions before an audience. If you produce nothing—and I assure you, some of us have tried that; there are Authors in Residence here who swear they'll never write anything again—they ask about your past work instead. Repeat as necessary until your time in hell is over."

Carlson frowned. "All of that sounds pretty standard."

"Oh, it's standard all right," Finn said, with bleak finality. "The Tchi have it down to a science."

"And this defeats people, how?"

"It defeats them by driving a stake through every creative impulse they ever had. Look. Remember Sandra Jaagin?"

Of course Carlson did. He'd shared a teaching fellowship, and for a while an apartment, with her at the University of New Kansas. It was there, in fact, that she'd sold her first novel: also there that Carlson, whose own career had not been going well at the time, had burst into a jealous tantrum that turned everything sour for the few weeks their relationship still had to live. He had always wanted to run into her again, so he could apologize. "The Tchi made her stop writing?"

"She's well and truly blocked. These days she goes on a lot of long walks. And then there's Vera Lugoff."

Carlson remembered Vera from several previous writing conferences. She was an odd twig of a woman, poorly socialized even by the sometimes generous standards afforded fiction writers, who specialized in the production of epic doorstops about virginal frontier women and the shaggy-maned, bare-chested louts who loved them. The supreme sexual act for the couples inhabiting any Vera Lugoff novel seemed to be standing atop one windswept crag or another, and proclaiming their love in endless three-page sentences crammed with enough metaphors to make her pages sticky. Vera spoke much the same way, and always radiated scorn when her five-hundred word declarations of nothing in particular failed to produce sustained replies in the same prose style. Carlson had never known another writer so much in love with her own work, or any other whose ego had seemed more impervious to criticism. He squeaked: "She's here?"

"She's here, nested flashbacks and all. The Tchi flew her in three months ago. And she was game all right: she flounced in, and read her first excerpt in a fit of high eloquence capable of flattening even the most demanding human audience in either satisfaction or sheer dumbfounded amazement. And guess what?"

"What?"

"It took less than a dozen sessions with the Tchi to break her. She's stopped writing. She just stays inside her bungalow and weeps, saying that she'll never write a word again."

"Vera said that? *Vera?!*"

"Vera," Finn confirmed. "We've had suicide attempts, outbreaks of alcoholism, buzzpop abuse and other arcane addictions, perfectly good manuscripts fed to deletion programs, one nervous breakdown that left its victim declaring himself a mushroom, and at least a dozen talented writers who have found themselves unable to add a single word to their online files in weeks or months. Lord alone knows how many of them will produce again. I'm stronger than most, and my muse may have fallen down the well for good."

Carlson was horrified, intrigued, terrified, and defiant, all at once. The main reason he wasn't actually forewarned is that he was also a professional writer, which is to say he'd spent much of his life listening to all the learned voices, ranging from his parents to his ex-wives to the grey-beared eminences who had plowed this ground before him, who had advised him of doom if he allowed his life to take this course. So instead of asking Finn for further details, he just ventured, "That won't happen to me."

And Finn exploded. Almost literally; a few additional grams per square millimeter pressure against the inside of his skull and he might have left most of his cerebrum plastered against the skimmer walls. As it is, his head bulged. "Oh, so you think you're better than us."

"Oh, come on, I never said that, it's just that you've always been hypersensitive to criticism—"

"Oh, that's it," Finn laughed. "And you're not? Forgive me for thinking otherwise! I know you're better than us! You can't be broken by the same forces breaking the rest of us mere mortals! I'll just cease doubting you and permit you to enter the lair of beasts without further warning!"

The goggling Carlson said, "I never—"

"No, to hell with you. I'll just let you get up before all those Tchi and learn for yourself. It's just about the only form of entertainment us poor scribes have around here!"

• • • •

At first, the press conference didn't seem any more, or any less, grim than most other public appearances of Carlson's experience.

There were the Tchi, of course: disconcerting enough when encountered in human space, where most people operating outside diplomatic circles rarely encountered more than one or two at a time. As on the transport, there was something about the way they raised their eyebrows, or curled their lips, at even the slightest human utterance, that had always made Carlson wonder if his deodorant had failed: and when they performed their silent derision act in public, it was a little like having his fragile sense of self-worth pelted with invisible foam-rubber mallets. But Carlson had spoken at many other colleges in his career, including many which catered exclusively to the children of the entitled and privileged: he was well acquainted with the hostile blank stares of those who had never heard of him, those who had never had any interest in hearing of him, and those who resented him for their University's insistence in believing that they might want to hear of him. He found nothing in the many rows filled with Tchi grimaces he could not connect to those prior experiences.

Too, there was the comfort to be found in the presence of his colleagues: not just Finn, who stood in the back of the chamber, grinning nastily as he waited for the carnage to follow, and Vera Lugoff, who had affected an ancient widow's veil out of mourning for whatever she thought the Tchi had done to her, but also a number of individuals Carlson actually liked and respected. He was particularly pleased to see Sandra Jaagin: she was many years older, like himself, but showed the signs of regular rejuvenation treatments, and seemed kilometers removed from the broken woman Finn had described: she even smiled at him from her spot at the back of the room. Only the sudden urgency that flared in her eyes, when the Tchi moderator Dr. Flei Garkh stepped up to the podium to introduce him, gave Carlson another frisson of fear.

Garkh licked his miniscule lips with the distaste of a creature who had just found something moving on them, and said, "Today we are pleased to have with us the eminent Hom.Sap author, Brian Carlson, a man who exemplifies the state of the art insofar as it applies to his species. He is, in fact, a multiple award winner, demonstrating that his race judges him as near or at the top of their version of the quality scale. Carlson has joined our acclaimed Author-In-Residence program, where his regular contributions will provide us with vivid, and repeated, demonstrations of Hom.Sap preferences in story construction. He has agreed, in fact, to open today's conference with a reading from a representative sample of his work. Mr. Carlson?"

Defiant applause from every human being except Everett Finn, who kept his arms folded in angry challenge.

Well, to hell with him.

Carlson made the usual opening remarks about the great honor of being permitted to represent his species, and the tremendous importance of cross-cultural exchange, and the great hope that this might support even better relations between their two great species in the future, give me a break, blah, blah, blah.

Then he activated his hytex link and began to read.

Carlson had built his reputation on two mutually exclusive genres: interspecies thrillers, in which he concocted clockwork interstellar conspiracies involving intricate alliances between alien races both actual and invented, which if left unchecked by his valiant heroes and heroines threatened to wreak horrific carnage of world-destroying proportions; and heartwarming bucolic adventures about a bookish young boy coming of age in the watery pastures of the ocean world Greeve. Both stretched the bounds of reader credulity, in the first case because his elephantine conspiracies never imploded out of poor management or internal rot, like most conspiracies on that scale, and in the second case because the young hero of his Greeve series, widely recognized to be a version of Carlson himself, hadn't aged a day despite more than thirty volumes detailing events that ate up an average of one year apiece.

Carlson's latest opus, of which he was inordinately fond, belonged to neither fictive universe: it was a truth-based love story involving a Cylinked boy and girl, who having rewired themselves into a new gestalt personality, now find a shared yen for each others' exes. It was an excerpt from this newest work that he read to the assembled Tchi, utilizing the expert command of accent and idiom that had once led him to consider a secondary career as a supporting actor in neurec drama.

Carlson projected. He drank in the silence of his audience and read it as appreciation. He lost himself in the story he had written, saw his audience in there with him, and for a few fleeting moments was not a fictioneer of undeniable but sadly limited gifts but a god glorying in the richness of the universe he had created.

He finished to polite hissing.

This he'd been warned about: it was the Tchi equivalent of applause. He took it as intended, and responded in the preferred manner, by pressing his palm against his forehead and rocking his head to and fro, all the while thinking, *I don't know what Finn's talking about, this isn't that bad.*

Then came the questions.

"Mr. Carlson: the sun in your world's sky, what is its surface temperature?"

Carlson blinked. "I don't know. It's a warm world, though. The habitable regions are high tropical, by human standards. I describe the weather there in detail—"

"Mr. Carlson: Would you know its high altitude weather systems?"

"No. But neither would she. The schools—"

"Mr. Carlson: she eats with a utensil you call a fork. Four curved tines at the end of a handle. Would you happen to know why four tines became the standard, and not six?"

"That's deep background," Carlson said. "I suppose I—"

"Mr. Carlson: the female you write of. You say she has freckles. These are local variations in skin pigmentation, aggravated by ultra-violet radiation. You say that they fan out across both cheeks. What side had more? The left or the right?"

Carlson was just beginning to realize he'd entered hell. "Both cheeks were equally freckled."

"Mr. Carlson: would a medical examination confirm the accuracy of this count?"

"Human beings don't count their freckles," he said.

"As the author, Mr. Carlson, it was up to you to design her facial features. Announcing that she was freckled without offering a precise count amounts to abdicating your responsibility toward your readers. You must have a precise count."

"I don't."

"And yet you know for a fact that she had an equal number of freckles on both cheeks?"

"More or less!"

"More or less is not equal, Mr. Carlson. So you contradict yourself."

"I haven't—"

"We have noted similar inadequacies in the imagination of your fellow humans, Mr. Finn: their fictive creations deflate like empty vessels upon any rigorous examination. This is even true of your so-called classics. Are you familiar with the works of your famed earther, Victor Hugo?"

Hugo had been one of Carlson's earliest influences; he had written several papers on the man's work, had indeed spent a couple of semesters teaching it to bored University students who had needed two months of special orientation before they could appreciate the conventions and mores of an earthbound, pre-diaspora economy. He didn't have the hear the snotty intonation in the Tchi's voice to know that the bastard knew it. "Yes?"

"On the day Jean Valjean is released from prison, what is the humidity?"

"I don't know."

"Exactly how many insects infest his clothing?"

"I don't know."

"What is the state of his periodontic health?"

"I don't know!" he shouted. "It's irrelevant!"

"Irrelevant," the Tchi said. "Irrelevant."

"Yes, dammit! You don't need to know everything that's happening on every single centimeter of his body to get swept up in the story, or to understand its underlying theme of social injustice!"

There was a pause. The Tchi sat silent, the collective force of their disapproval washing over him like a tidal surge. They didn't have to say anything; anything they put into actual words would have been superfluous.

Predictably, inevitably, without any gesture toward mercy, the words arrived, planting themselves one after another, with the pitiless finality of gravestones.

"So you admit," the Tchi said, "that human authors are inadequate?"

The earth cooled. The continents formed. Life rose from the deep, was wiped out by the asteroid strike, and continued in bold new forms. The Renaissance came and went. The stars went black and died. Hell filled with souls and put out a NO VACANCY sign. Time stopped as all creation contracted to the size of a dot.

The Q & A seemed to last one full hour after that.

* * * *

For Carlson, light returned to the universe later that evening, and the wine, cheese and condolence party the various human writers trapped in the hell of Tchi academia threw in their compound, to welcome the latest inmate of their shared hell.

It was not a bad place, as torture chambers go. In its own way, it was quite beautiful. The Tchi had built a circle of cottages around a glen wooded with popular species from human worlds, and landscaped to provide walking paths and shade and plenty of sunlight for humans who liked that sort of thing. Maybe they did want to be good hosts. Or maybe they were sadists who realized gardens and sunlight could be torment to people already driven into despair.

The welcome party was held in the clearing. Carlson had already endured the sympathy of several mystery novelists, a memoirist, a satirist, and a writer of epistolary fiction once notorious for couching the letters his characters had written to one another in untranslated binary code.

Carlson had been told not to worry overmuch about a bunch of Tchi assholes; as long as his colleagues knew he was a good writer, and he knew himself to be a good writer, and he would one day be free to return to human space where at least one person in a couple of hundred thousand still had some use for good writers, he should not allow the Tchi mission to destroy him any more impact than a light spring rain.

Of course, he would have to endure a questioning just as brutal one week from now. And one week after that.

And just about everybody who offered him sympathy averted their eyes when he countered by asking them how their own writing was going. Their respective muses were all, if not shackled, then bruised to the point where putting pen to paper (or keystrokes to electron template, or neurally transmitted impulses to hytexual database, or whatever) was too painful to bear.

The evening did not seem about to substantially improve when he recognized the next sympathetic face in line. He completely forgot the acrimonious nature of their parting and leaped up to say hello. "Sandra!"

She shared his embrace. "Brian. I'm so sorry. I would have warned you if I could."

"That's all right," he said, grinning with genuine happiness for the first time since the press conference. "How the hell are you doing?"

"Could be worse," she said. "I haven't been able to finish anything for months, but at least I have a sense of humor about it. You're looking good. Fatter, but still good."

"You too. Except for the fatter part." Back when Brian had first known and loved her, Sandra had been a slender, elfin thing with close-cropped black hair and the terrible habit some women have of punctuating every statement with a self-deprecating giggle, as if the mere act of speaking her mind deserved apology. Back then she'd defied her natural shyness with outrageous fashions, including those with animated holographic patterns and at least one that sounded a buzzer and turned transparent at randomly-generated intervals. She'd lost some of the slenderness, but the added weight balanced her face and made her more a woman than a waif; and the sunny yellow tunic she wore now enhanced from her features rather than distracting from them, like some of the things she'd worn in the old days.

Without wanting to, he felt a moment of deep, heartbreaking nostalgia for their times together. "God, but it's good to see you!"

"Wish I could say the same," she said, sending his spirits deeper into the basement. They bounced back a little with her next words. "You really do deserve better than this. Have you figured out, or has anybody bothered to explain, just what's going on here?"

"Ummm. Not really. Finn tried to warn me before the Q & A, but we butted heads and he never got around to finishing."

"Then it falls to me," she said, and grabbed his hand. "Come on, we'll find a quiet corner."

Once upon a time, Sandra would have died before presume to guide anybody but a child by the hand; she hadn't had the self-confidence to presume herself a fit guide to lead anybody anywhere. Now she was like a bulldozer, expertly carving her way past the throng of inebriates in tweed, deflecting the one or two who still hadn't offered Carlson their sympathies. The last one she evaded was Vera, who wore the look of a ghostly bride glimpsed in the upper windows of some Victorian mansion; and it was a good thing Sandra was able to spare him the encounter, because the one overriding quality in Vera's eyes was defeat, and Carlson didn't think he was in any state to be doused in any more of it.

The refuge Sandra found was a stone bench by a narrow brook, the rushing water just loud enough to serve as welcome white noise, obliterating the chatter of the other authors in residence. She sat him down, then took her own place beside him, and began, "I'm half-inclined to let you knock your head against the wall until it becomes obvious. You were a real jerk, way back when."

"I know," he said. "I've been meaning to get back in touch with you and tell you that. I'm sorry."

She studied his face. "Why didn't you?"

"I had a good excuse."

"Which was?"

Carlson spread his hands. "Cowardice."

She showed no surprise, just nodded, and looked away. "I figured as much. But you had a good heart, and that's rare enough among real people, let alone writers, so I'll spare you some of the confusion you must be feeling right now. Have you ever actually read any Tchi literature?"

With something like shame, Carlson realized that it had never occurred to him, not even when in the months between the invitation and the embarkation of the Tchi shuttle. "Uh, no."

"Then you don't know what they consider a good novel, right?"

"Well, I assumed . . ."

"That's right. You assumed that just because they invited you to be the guest of honor it was because they wanted to honor you."

"It usually follows."

She sighed. "How long have you been on the lecture circuit, Brian? Haven't you learned yet that sometimes they hire you because they want to do the exact opposite?"

Carlson remembered a small college he'd visted on the wheelworld New London. There'd been a symposium dedicated to his work. He'd wandered in, expecting kudos, and found that he main subject of discussion had turned out to be the flatness of his characters as shaped by the psychosexual inadequacies of the author. After three hours he'd become more evidence in the popular stereotype of novelists as raving egomaniacs who drink. He had sworn never to accept such an invitation again. But the idea of being honored by an actual alien race had overcome his misgivings, and . . .

. . . and for the first time in his life, he now actually felt the sensation novelists mean when they reference a sinking feeling. "What are they up to?"

"Tchi don't like human beings. They consider us violent, uneducated philistines, with a barely evolved sense of aesthetics and a pop culture that debases us and every other alien race that has ever developed an appreciation for any of our work. The curriculum of their Human Studies program is entirely devoted to reinforcing that thesis. When they invite our best writers here—at least, those who aren't warned off—they do so with the specific purpose of humiliating us with the inadequacies of our literary traditions as judged by the specific criteria of their own standards. In short, you're here to be held up as a negative example. To be humiliated. No story you write, no matter how good, can possibly meet with their approval. I mean, *no* story. They're particularly fond of ripping apart our classics. What they do to Jane Austen alone is enough to make a strong woman cry."

He gulped. "Why do we sit still for it?"

"Because we have no choice. We signed the contracts. We accepted their honoraria. We agreed to come and face their questions. If any of us refuse to cooperate, the penalties are more than any working writer could ever afford to pay; they'd end up owning everything you've ever written and everything you ever would write in perpetuity, giving them the right to drive your reputation even further into the grave publishing annotated editions that exist only to support their perception of you as dishonest, demented, shallow, untalented, and unTchian in every way." She grimaced. "Do that and you'll be buried. I'd die before I let them do that to *Cold Victory*."

That had been Sandra's first novel, a portrait if a character secretly based on her remote and disapproving father. He remembered her saying that she'd cried herself blind while writing it. He remembered the acclaim it had received on publication, the lump it had raised in his own throat, the very real sense of closure it had given her. And then he realized that the questions the Tchi asked her must have included contemptuous ones about *that very book*, and how she would have had to sit and take them, on a weekly basis. Anger, the very real anger of a novelist faced with societies of evil critics, overcame him, and he said, "They can't be allowed to get away with this."

She snorted. "Oh, Brian. How can you stop them?"

"I haven't figured that out yet. But I'll defeat them. Don't you worry. I'll shut them down and leave them begging for mercy. This I swear."

Sandra just stared at him, blinking, for several seconds, before laughing out loud. "I almost believe you."

"You should believe me. I'm serious."

She touched a fingertip to his lips. "I know you are. But this is their world, their rules, their aesthetic. You can't write the kind of prose they like, and you can't make them like yours. It's a fool's game."

"Then I'm a fool," he said recklessly. "But I will defeat them. I will."

She sighed, looked upon with a special kind of affection that looked like it did not want to cross the boundaries of pity, and gave him a chaste kiss on the cheek. "If you ever actually manage to do what you just said, you'll be my hero for life."

"Really?" he said. "Enough to be given a second chance?"

She was dubious, but desperate enough to consider it. "Sure. Why not."

And this, of course, was a challenge no heterosexual male novelist could have refused.

* * * *

The next day, his head pounding from all the drinks pressed into his hands by fellow writers eager to see another get as sloppily drunk as they'd seen themselves get, Carlson left the compound of the humiliated and found his way to the University's Main Library, where the Tchi on duty took one look at him and inquired, with just the right degree of scorn and condescension, whether he was really in the right building? Didn't the works here have subtexts and subtleties no human being could possibly understand?

He smiled and handed the withering snot a list of three titles alleged to be the greatest novels in Tchi history. The snot told him they were available via hytex link. Carlson smiled and said, "Aaaah, but the sheer sensory experience of holding the books in my hands, as I soak up the brilliance . . . !"

It required an interlibrary transmittal, and consultation with the director of the Human Studies program, but by late that afternoon the Tchi authorized the replication of three volumes of in approved Mercantile translations, printed and bound in the format Carlson always preferred when he read novels on paper.

This was a mistake.

None of the novels were shorter than three thousand pages.

Grimacing as much from the weight as the prospect of reading these behemoths, but adopting the fiction of happy anticipation, Carlson lugged them back to his bungalow and spent all of that night beginning the first and by reputation most honored among them.

After six pages he went back to the beginning, unwilling to believe that the story was unfolding as it seemed to be. Confirming the awful truth, and feeling more and more despair by the time he bulled his way past page one hundred, he rejected the impulse to feed the damned thing to a fire and forced himself onward, ever onward, paragraph by paragraph, tedious line by tedious line.

Somehow, heroically, he reached page two hundred that night, having already misdiagnosed the pain of getting that far as a dozen separate strokes. Before he collapsed, he flipped the remaining pages all the way to the end, confirming the awful truth.

In the morning he knocked on Sandra's door. "Want to take a walk?"

She was frowsy-haired, wearing a cloth robe and drinking something hot from a cup. "Depends. Given up on defeating them yet?"

"No," he said. "Actually, I think I might have a handle on the situation."

She raised an eyebrow, brushed a sleepy tangle of hair away from her opposite cheek. "I must say. Heroic fantasy's a new genre for you, Bri."

"No, I'm serious," he insisted. "I just need to clarify some things. Come on, take a walk with me." When she hesitated still further, he added, "Unless you'd rather stay home and try to write . . ."

The terrible truth about novelists is that precious few of them, given a choice of activities, would rather stay home and try to write. Faced with a way out, Sandra moved faster than any whirlwind.

An hour later, the two of them had settled beside the same stream where they'd last spoken two nights before. They'd talked about everything but Carlson's plan for a counter-offensive, but now Sandra had kicked off her shoes so she could dangle her feet in the water, and Carlson, who required all his might to ignore the sight of the sun glinting on her hair, needed to talk business or die. "I started reading *A Thousand Futilities* last night."

She coughed, hard. "Oh, Brian. I'm so sorry. How far did you get?"

"Two hundred pages. Skimmed the rest."

"That's further than I got. I think Vera got to fifty. The poor thing's never been the same."

"I have two other Tchi classics," Carlson told her, "but a quick glance at those makes me fear for my sanity if I continued. Still, it remains possible that the equivalent of Dickens or Dumas or Hugo or even Quantum Cloud remains somewhere in the Tchi canon, so it would save me a whole lot of pain if you did me the favor of fact-checking my conclusions."

She gave him a thumb's up, threw her head back so her face could catch the sun, and said, "Shoot."

He said, "As near as I can figure from my exposure to the greatest novel in Tchi history, and I must admit from using the hytex to consult academic papers our own best universities have written about their canon, Tchi fiction has never been about plot, or character, or even theme. It's about nested parentheses."

She swirled the water with her toe. "Interesting way of putting it."

"Historically, the typical Tchi novel has always been centered on the elaborations of the most miniscule subject matter they can concoct. Let's say, a vase bearing a single flower. What kind of flower? They describe that. Where was it picked? The describe the region and its entire economic development. What kind of vase? They describe the design, go into several pages about how the school of artists that developed it. In further chapters they talk about the clay it was fashioned from, and why potters find that clay preferable to that available down the road. Then they talk about the table. Don't get me started on how they go on about tables. Then they go into describing the room, and every last detail about every single furnishing, and maybe, if they want to be really daring, an actual person sitting on a chair somewhere in that room. They describe that person and going into every last detail about that person's genealogy. The one thing they won't do, ever, is have that person get up and get himself involved in an actual story, because that's gauche, that's a betrayal of the kind of subtlety they prefer. And besides, if they did that, then they'd be likely to forget some more important details like the precise amount of fraying on the local area rug. It's this layering, this obsessive accumulation of detail, the more mundane the better, that the Tchi intelligentsia consider art. Am I correct so far?"

Sandra shuddered. "You are. And to think I used to have problems absorbing Joyce and Proust."

But Carlson was still warming up. "Tchi novelists seek to provide so much detail of a single static moment that the rest of the world can be inferred, whereas even the most leisurely human novelists move their narratives through time and sketch in only enough detail to enrich the story, an amount that must by necessity assume some details extraneous and therefore safe to omit. A Tchi writer, invited to a symposium like this, would be able to describe the precise contents of a desk drawer in the home of an academic living across the street from a house where his novel takes place; and it's not the kind of thing that can be faked, because if he doesn't put that detail in his book he will be asked that question not once or twice but every single time his book is discussed in public. That's why their most respected books are all two thousand pages long. That's why they get longer when they're annotated by academics. In short, their platonic ideal as far as fiction is concerned is a bludgeon too heavy to lift and too motionless to endure. Do I have all of this correct?"

Sandra kicked at the burbling water, creating a silvery arc that achieved beauty of its own before collapsing forever. "Yes, you do. But you can't fight that, Brian. It's their world, their aesthetic standards. If you ever tell them to their faces that you think their literature sucks, they'll just blame it on your coarse human sensibilities and your inability to appreciate their finer subtleties."

"Oh, I know that," Carlson said.

"And you can't imitate what they do, either. Trust me, several of us have tried. Write ten pages of a novel in the true Tchi tradition, and your eyes will cross. Write fifty and you'll want to kill yourself. Write a hundred and you may never finish anything publishable in human space ever again. Manage to finish one—as one of us did, a couple of years ago—and you'll find yourself unable to defend it to the extent they require; try as you might, they'll find the contradictions, or the holes, and trumpet your failure even louder. You'll have tortured yourself for no reason."

"I know that too," Carlson said. "And I have absolutely no intention of trying."

She contemplated his expression for several seconds, frowned as she registered the confidence in his eyes, and splashed the water again. "But you said you can defeat them."

He grinned. "I know I can."

"In Juje's name, how?"

He picked up a rock in tossed it into the brook, enjoying the ker-plunk of the splashdown, taking special pleasure in imagining that the running water was the Tchi literary tradition and the stone his own special contribution, still to come. "By using their own nature against them.—Come on. I think it's time that we go talk to the others."

◦ ◦ ◦ ◦

Two days later, it was Everett Finn's turn in the hot seat. As usual, he'd failed to produce anything new in the interim since his last weekly evisceration, so the Tchi had exercised the contractual clause that prevented the human writers in residence from simply abdicating their responsibilities and programmed a discussion on one of his past case: in this case a very sweet little autobiographical story about the ten-year-old

Everett's first space walk. Finn had won a minor literary award for the piece, and still had some affection for it, though he now considered it juvenilia. The Tchi had spent the greater part of three hours demanding a full dissertation on orbital mechanics, down to the precise volume of canned atmosphere that bled into space when the airlock he'd used opened to vacuum. Finn kept to his usual strategy of sullen monosyllabic answers until the Q & A was almost over, at which point, as arranged, he allowed his voice to break and broke down sobbing into cupped hands.

The gathered Tchi took this with remarkable aplomb; it was, after all, the reaction they demanded. Garkh said, "Are you all right, Mr. Finn?"

Finn shook his head. "N-no. You're right. My work is sloppy and half-assed. It's not good enough. It'll never be good enough."

"Are you then changing your position, and conceding the inferiority of the human literary tradition?"

"Y-yes," Finn said. "*I'm so ashamed.*" He wailed and stormed out, covering his eyes as a veritable font of tears gushed down his cheeks.

The Tchi did not see him slow down as he passed Carlson, fix his long-time rival with a glare of undying hatred, and mutter, "You better be right."

Nor did the assorted Tchi academics see the similar eye contact when every other human writer in the program, attending their own Q & A sessions over the course of the next week, succumbed to similar bursts of overwhelming faux-despair. It wasn't all anger; some of the hysterical breakdowns the Tchi witnessed, and failed to properly recognize, were actual hysterical breakdowns, of the mirthful variety. No Tchi were present the one fine evening that Vera Lugoff had a little too much to drink and giggled nonstop for close to an hour, wailing, "I'm *so ashamed*," with a level of delight that rendered her intoxication redundant. There were lots of hangovers, that next week, lots: again, nothing unusual at a novelists conference, but the revels themselves were less the usual pits of auctorial despair than wild celebration at the prospect of striking back at their tormentors.

The Tchi could not be blamed for suspecting that something was up, and were even more than typically offensive in their questioning when Carlson's turn came again.

• • • •

Following the lead the others had set on his instruction, Carlson failed to produce any new work by the deadline, and therefore had to endure the savaging of a favorite old work of his, which included questions like, "Exactly how many hair follicles did Suzie have?" and, "What was Professor Clump's blood pressure at this time?"

It took everything Carlson had to sit through the interrogation, but he did, surprising his hosts by not pretending to break down.

Instead, he rubbed his chin thoughtfully. "You know, you're right. You're absolutely right. The human literary tradition is inferior to yours. But it's not the only one that could stand improvement."

A murmur rippled through the gathered Tchi literati. "Specify," Garkh said.

"I've been reading some of your great Classics, like *A Thousand Futilities*, and *Anarchy* and *The Dust in the Purg-Farmer's Restroom*, and while I'm astounded at their brilliance and their wealth of detail, it occurs to me that your canon lacks the fresh, cleansing spirit of innovation necessary to keep any great art form alive. I believe that the addition of allusion and implication, wielded by an expert hand, can drive a volume with as much nested detail as even the greatest Tchi novels of all time, in but a fraction of the space. Indeed, now that my eyes have been opened, I believe that I'm about to produce a work as meritorious as even your immortal Vlurkh-Bom's *Nostril*, and that I'm going to fill it with all the verve and emotional truth and compelling relevance that have always been so praised among our own great writers. In short, give me one week and I promise you that I will come up with something capable of doing the great names of the Tchi literary tradition proud."

The room erupted. There were cries of "impossible!" and "one week?" and "a human?" and so on, not to mention a few scattered boos, but Carlson had expected that, and he continued to stand firm, his head held high, his chin outthrust as far as his rather flabby chin could thrust. In the human gallery at the back of the room, Everett Finn scowled, Vera Lugoff coughed into a handkerchief, and Sandra Jaagin beamed, her faith in the enterprise now so overpowering that it was enough to dispel all the dark clouds of negativity emitted by their combined patrons and tormentors.

Resisting the urge to wink may have been the single most self-sacrificial moment of Carlson's life.

Eventually, the hubbub died. Garkh emerged from a huddle with some of his colleagues, strode back to the podium, and sneered, "One week. You say that you can best our greatest literary works in one week."

"Yes," said Carlson. "I believe I can."

"We do not believe it, Brian Carlson. No human novelist has the brilliance or the subtlety to pull off such an unprecedented feat. But you have dictated the terms of your own challenge. We will meet back here in one week, where you will either read a composition as remarkable as your claims, or admit the inherent inferiority of not only your own narrative traditions but also the very creative potential of your species."

"Agreed," Carlson said, with reckless abandon. "On the condition that you put all responsibility for that question on my shoulders. Whether I succeed or fail, you must pay my colleagues the remainder of their honoraria, release them from the remainder of their contracts, and provide their transportation back to their respective points of origin."

Another colloquy, and Garkh returned again. "Agreed. With the understanding that by cutting off all further debate you allow the entire literary reputation of your species to rest on your own inadequate shoulders."

Carlson could barely contain his mirth. "In that case I had better get started. Thank you for your time." He stepped away from the podium, and bowed, and strode down the center aisle, pausing at the exit so the rest of the human writers in attendance could join what had now become a mass exodus.

Everett Finn, who had maneuvered himself close to him, repeated his previous warning. "You had better be right."

Carlson kept his smile fixed. "Oh, shut up."

* * * *

The week that followed was an exercise in inexorably building tension, as the humans awaited the moment of truth and their hosts trumpeted the importance and the finality of the showdown to come.

Carlson didn't subject himself to much of what the Tchi media had to say about him, but he caught some of it by accident, and the big issue seemed to be just which of the culture's many superstar academics would eviscerate it with the cruelest eloquence. The snottiest of the bunch were as famous as sports stars, their visages captured on collectable cards sold in packs along with a mucus-like gel the Tchi prized for its sweetness and chewability. The upcoming destruction of Carlson's reputation was such an eagerly-awaited occasion that it had even drawn a number of the field's all-stars out of retirement, prompting much speculation over whether the most incisive condemnations would come from masters like Khludt and Kyael, or such upstarts as Phyeyilii.

Nobody on the Tchi side seemed to think that Carlson's upcoming opus could possibly be anything but a disaster. Which was pretty much how Carlson wanted it. He didn't talk about it much with the rest of the human writers, with the exception of one conversation between he had with Sandra over waffles.

It was, it followed, the last thing he wanted to talk about, since it had been years since she'd made him waffles.

But she said, "You know they're lying in wait for you, right? That they're pulling out every stop to make this humiliating."

He had been in the act of pouring his maple syrup, a moment that had possessed significant sensual pleasure all by itself, since it had been years since he'd indulged his famous passion for maple syrup and found extreme significance in the very fact that Sandra had managed to obtain some for him, here on the Tchi homeworld. "We've talked about this, my love. The more effort they put into destroying, the further I can throw them with my own brilliant rhetorical ju-jitsu."

"I'm just saying that you don't have to go through this just to impress me."

His fork hovered over the treasure on his plate. "Do you really think I'm doing this just to impress you?"

She colored. "Well, aren't you? At least a little?"

Carlson put down his fork while it still remained unwaffled. "I'm crazy about you, Sandra. I'll always be crazy about you, and I'll always count driving you away as the second worst mistake I ever made, directly behind that liability clause on my second novel contract. And it's a near thing, even there. But if you think I'm doing this for you, I'm wrong. I'm doing this for Shakespeare, Dickens, Twain, Ibsen, Hemingway, Steinbeck, Vonnegut, Rowling, X'uffasch, Dawntreader, and everybody else those people have locked outside the city gates and thrown garbage at. I'm doing this because I want past those gates so the trash starts landing on the right heads for a change and because I happen to be the one who thought of a way to build a big wooden horse in the shape of a manuscript. Impressing you is just a wonderful added benefit."

Sandra's lips moved without emitting sound. Then she found her voice and said, "Eat up. Your waffles are getting cold."

He picked up the fork again, suppressing a helpless grin.

That was about as good as it got, until the day itself.

* * * *

On the day itself the final confrontation was held, not in the modest seminar room of the earlier Q & A sessions, but in a vast off-campus auditorium, lit by balloons filled with tumescent vapor, and filled to the very last seat with Tchi luminaries radiating waves of full-bore disapproval. The stage was furnished not only by the lectern where Carlson was expected to stand, but also by two long tables occupied by several of the venerable names Carlson had learned about from the collectable cards, their expressions already dour and puckered and suggestive of long unpleasant lives spent scraping disagreeable substances from the soles of their shoes.

Garkh absented himself from the carnage being plotted on the dais and strode to the lectern, where he was greeted by polite applause from the two rows of gathered human writers and energetic hissing from the remainder of the great hall's population. He said, "My fellow sentients, we are gathered here today to judge the work of the human being Brian Carlson, who has claimed himself capable of redeeming the sloppy and barely intelligible prose of his species with a work that incorporates and improves upon the finest accomplishments of our own. He has refused to submit his work for prior review, saying only that he can present it in its entirety this evening. If, like me, you doubt that this cannot be anything but proof of his self-deluded inadequacy, you will humor his madness in coming here with a reception as warm as the one you have given me. Gentlebeings, the human being Brian Carlson."

More applause. More hissing. Carlson strode to the podium, waited for the tumult to die down, and scanned the first row for the pair of eyes most important to him.

Sandra gave him a thumbs up.

So did Everett Finn, who had taken the seat beside her. His poor opinion of Carlson had not changed, but he knew enough to root for his team, and had wished Carlson luck earlier this morning, with a final, begrudged, *Gotta hand it to you, Brian. You sure do know how to go out in style.*

Carlson smiled at both of them, communicating the absolute confidence he felt at this moment, then adopted his academic face and said, "Good evening, everybody.

"My name is Brian Carlson.

"I'm here, on this occasion, because I believe that I've completed a work that combines the vibrant narrative power of the best human fiction with the all-inclusive detail of the best Tchi work: a work that by implication captures every salient feature of an entire imaginary world, from the smallest blade of grass to the jagged peaks of its most majestic, snow-capped mountains. It is a world as richly imagined as the ones described in such pivotal Tchi works as *Pebble* and *Sleeping Fungus* and *Intestinal Distress*, yet as filled with drama and conflict as the greatest works on the Hom.Sap bookshelf: a book that has been pared down to its most essential facts, that nevertheless contains all the others as subtext and implication. I feel entirely justified in resting the reputation of all my race's finest accomplishments on this, the most important story I've ever written. It's called *The Rock*, and it's my supreme honor to present it to you, my colleagues, for the very first time."

He took a deep breath, allowed the silence to build build build, and then placed the manuscript on the lectern before him.

"*The Rock* by Brian T. Carlson.

"*The Rock*," he said, again pausing, imparting all the possibilities inherent in that one sad moment of silence, "*sat imbedded in mud beneath a gray, twilit sky.*"

Pause Pause Pause.

You could hear a pin drop.

Then Carlson took a deep breath and added, "The end."

Then he stepped away from the podium and bowed, waiting for the inevitable tidal wave of disbelief and rage.

It didn't take long. All at once, the audience exploded, humans with awestruck cheers and Tchi with helpless astonishment. One of the learned figures on the dais performed a perfect spit-take. Another reared back so violently he hit the back of his head on the backdrop. Unprepared for the suddenness of their cue, they glared at each other and at him and at the audience before getting it together enough to pelt him with incredulous questions.

"What?"

"Is that it?"

"Is that the whole thing?"

"Is this a joke?"

"Have you taken leave of your senses, man?"

"What kind of world does this take place on?"

"Is it inhabited?"

"Is there a civilization?"

"What's the average yearly rainfall?"

"Is this a big rock or a small rock?"

"How many grams does it weigh?"

"Is it igneous, sedimentary, or compound?"

"Are there ants on it?"

"How many ants?"

"What's the precise chemical breakdown of that mud?"

"How deep is it?"

"Is the water potable?"

"You haven't answered my question about the ants!"

And so on, and so forth, a veritable torrent of angry questions, pelting Carlson's bowed shoulders with all the force of a light spring rain.

Aware that his enemies thought they already saw their own victory on the horizon, when that prize was his the instant he elected to grasp it, Carlson basked in the moment, reflecting that his colleagues should have been able to do what he was about to do, as soon as they became aware of the trap they'd fallen into; certainly, storytellers had taken the same out since the first caveman told the first mammoth-hunting anecdote around the first fire, and writers had been performing the same trick at academic conferences every since. For some, it had even been the entire basis of their careers. It should have been just as obvious, for those trapped here on the Tchi homeworld. Instead, Sandra and the others had acted like writers confronted by other writers, never once considering that the true solution to their woes had always rested in taking the traditional Out so favored by writers confronted by academics and critics.

And yet it was simple. By the end of this day, Garkh and the others would be competing with each other, to answer the very same questions they'd just been asking of him.

Content, already victorious in his heart, he waited for the weight of all those unanswerable questions to answer critical mass.

Then he fired his ultimate weapon.

He gave the learned figures on the dais the most incredulous look he could muster and demanded, "You mean to tell me you *don't know?*"

A SLIDE OF ASTONISHING DURATION

There was once upon a time a Super-Spy. You know his name. He said it often enough. We need another name for him and so we will call him John Bank.

Bank seduced a woman for information. She was of course a beautiful woman; somehow, in his life, all the women who possessed vital intelligence, or access to some impregnable installation, or the trust of some nefarious mastermind, or their own skill at dealing death and a willingness to have his back, all of them, were always drop-dead gorgeous, creatures of bright eyes and gleaming complexion who captured all the available light in any room they entered. They were profoundly evolved creatures, head and shoulders above their peers, approaching impossibility, without quite getting there.

This one had information he needed, and so Bank chatted her up at the casino, some casino somewhere whose guests uniformly sported formalwear and not t-shirts or warmup suits. His sparkling repartee matching her suggestive come-ons, and so within an hour they were in her suite, doing the deed on satin sheets, as foreplay to hard questions. She was also, as he suspected, an assassin, playing with him as a cat would a mouse, even as she told him everything he needed to know before the next bit. The idea was to lull him before she exercised her supernatural skill at knife-throwing. But he was not lulled. He left her unconscious on the bearskin rug before rappelling from the balcony, to the exotic streets far below; and this of course led to a car-chase across the historical district and a martial arts fight on a rooftop.

None of this was unusual for him. It was Thursday.

Later that night, penetrating the hidden stronghold of the criminal mastermind, he stepped in the wrong place and plunged through a trap door down a slide of astonishing duration, into a brightly lit chamber where the walls sprouted sawblades on extending poles and the floor was a grid emitting fountains of sulfuric acid, something that was also not exactly unusual for him, and he thought, "Not one of these again. Who thinks of these things, anyway? Who excavates the shafts? Who designs the machinery? Who constructs them? And how did he get into this line of business?"

Even after he escaped, even after he killed the villain in some witty manner, even after he defused the bomb and reported back to base, even after all that, these questions still weighed heavily on his heart.

● ● ● ●

The tavern of Master Olgarthe was a smoky hole so dark that it could only preferred by the blind or by those convenienced by the blindness of others. It occupied the most disreputable alley in the most disreputable section of a city with a higher murder rate than graduating college class, it sold substances that would have horrified the Medellin Cartel and it was the preferred watering hole of many whose services fell into the category of things too unpleasant for the Russian Mafia; any here, deals were made that resulted in spilled blood all over the world. Everybody kept their faces hidden beneath cigarette smoke and fedora brims, and it was said that at any given time approximately half the booths were occupied by people whose right hands were underneath the table, discreetly pointing Lugers at the crotches of the companions they drank with. Nobody used the bathrooms. Everybody stayed away from the alcoves where thick velvet curtains hid stranglers prepared to clutch them by the neck and draw them into the shadows. For years, Master Olgarthe had mulled offers to franchise.

Bank had for twenty minutes occupied a shadowy corner booth in the rear, half-hidden by a gigantic vase bearing a palm tree that he would not have been surprised to find out was rooted in some past, stashed corpse. He drank profusely. What he drank was irrelevant; the Super Spy had the knack of swilling enough hard liquor to put a lesser man into an alcoholic coma, and still somehow retain enough martial arts skill, inerrant marksmanship and capacity to think on his feet that he was, essentially, unkillable. His dark gaze still probed the room, taking note of the nefarious and the evil, the megalomaniacal and the merely sleazy, taking notes, even as they took note of him. Every instant was an exercise in plotting the order in which he would have had to slaughter them to make it to the door.

The fresco of desert sands on the far wall opened, revealing a passage hidden even to these reprobates whose lives were often dependent on familiarity with escape routes, and a woman known to him emerged silhouetted at the opening, visible only via the glint in her eyes and the sheen of captured candlelight across her honey-colored bangs. She naturally wore only a bikini and two dangling strands of cloth covering loins that Bank had already explored, between long shapely legs that accurately promised a panther's grace. Her nod was imperceptible and therefore instantly perceived by everyone in the room, even if all knew not to invade the passage without invitation, and certainly that it was likely not safe even then. None stood. None except Bank, who rose from his booth and slipped between the crowded tables, without ever removing his own gaze from that of the woman, whose lips bore a gloss the precise shade of spilled blood.

As he reached her, he said, "Yes?"

"He has agreed to receive you. Safe passage as long as you do not take liberties, or overstay your welcome. He has no fear of either, given who he is, but he despises rudeness."

"As do I," Bank replied.

His was a world where mortal enemies sometimes dined together, deploying the most elegant grace, before a planned battle to the death the following morning.

She led him up down a passage so narrow that they had to walk in single file, to a dead end that turned out not to be that because an almost invisible jog transformed it to intersection, into a larger chamber warehousing hundreds of crates containing God alone knew what obscenities, down a set of stairs, across a ledge abutting a tributary of the city sewer that required a kicking-aside of several indignant Norwegian rats, past another sliding panel and up another set of stairs to a set of drawn curtains that when parted revealed an elegant, if gloomy library with shelves that groaned with ten thousand volumes bound in matching red leather. Two enormous Caucasian Shepherds, growling softly, sat at attention in the room's far corners, regarding the Super-Spy as if contemplating the sweet joy of hearing his throat tear. One enormous fat man sat at one of two high-backed leather chair at the precise center of the room, cradling an open book with a gold-leaf spine, and it was this man who looked up, closed the volume and spoke in an accent that even Bank, who had been to well over a hundred countries, could not place. "Hello, sir."

"Good evening," Bank said.

"Sit with me, if you wish. I will not bite." The fat man looked past the Super-Spy to the beautiful woman who had been his guide through all those secret passages, and said, "Thank you, my Dear. You may leave us alone now."

She said, "As you wish," and departed, closing the curtains behind her.

Bank did not leave the threshold, but instead addressed the man in the high-backed chair. "You are Olgarthe?"

"I am."

"Where should I step to avoid your handiwork?"

"My dear man, every step you've taken since you left my club was a potential trigger for imminent destruction. You have stepped over pits of vipers, tiger cages, acid pools, and sheer drops that so deep that the narrowing angle of the inner walls was so gradual that you would have had time for multiple expletives before they met at the center over a razored opening the size of a bottle cap, the better to catch the blood. Trust me, if I wanted you dead before I heard you out you would not have come within a thousand meters of this sanctum. Please. Sit. I have honey cakes."

The Super-Spy entered the room, prepared for anything, the reflexes that had brought him alive through a thousand impossible situations both on fire and ready for anything, but also inert. He had long possessed the knack of sensing danger, but it could only work when danger came from a specific direction, and not when it loomed from all angles; and so it was wholly paralyzed now, raising his hackles only when the Caucasian Shepherds increased the intensity of their snarls. Even so, most observers would not have seen any signs of hesitation even as he made it to the opposing high-backed chair and out of politeness took one of the honey cakes, in specific the one on the fat man's plate.

The deliciousness of the cake reminded the Super Spy of the Zen parable about the monk, trapped halfway up a sheer cliff, with tigers at the summit at base, and a single sweet berry growing from the vine his weight is about to pull from the cliffside; the one that ends with the doomed monk tasting that berry and exclaiming, How sweet this is!

"Nice cake."

"Thank you," Olgarthe said. "I have servants to bake for me, but this treat is a private recipe and when offered my guests, guaranteed to have been made by these hands. The secret is browning the meringue."

Bank did not reach into his tuxedo jacket, pull out a little spiral-bound notebook, and record this information. He just nodded, putting this data aside as irrelevant.

"In any event," Olgarthe continued, "you have gone to extraordinary lengths to arrange this meeting. I have accepted the terms of our temporary armistice You may ask your questions."

Bank said, "That room in Marrakech, where the floor consisted of two sliding panels that slowly withdrew into the walls to arrange a swift drop into a pit of ravenous crocodiles: you designed that?"

"Yes. I did."

"And the one outside Prague, that first filled with five feet of seawater and then commenced replacing it, drop by drop, with hydrochloric acid: you designed that."

"Yes. I did."

"The one in Nairobi, where the walls were bricks made of ice that as they melted into the porous floor, gradually permitted the stone ceiling to descend closer and closer to crushing height: you designed that."

"My dear man, there is no reason to continue posing questions you already know the answer to. I designed them, and I designed all the others you have encountered, in your storied career. As well as many, many additional chambers that certain parties have installed in their private sanctums, solely for the benefit of those who stumble therein. I am, as the Americans would say, indeed 'that guy.'"

Bank said, "The organizations those rooms were built for were not all allied. Some were fervent enemies of the others, as engaged in battling one another as they were in carrying out their own separate agendas."

"True. My services have never included endorsement of the recipient causes."

"You are just a contractor."

"A merchant, sir. I daresay, perhaps even artist. I am the pre-eminent man in my field."

"Congratulations."

"Thank you. I got here by hard work, and, of course, by murdering the mentor who taught me."

Bank glanced about the elegantly-appointed room and said, "There are some here, I suppose."

"Several, sir. You will find that the very chair you sit in possesses a hidden trigger, responsive to me, that will plunge you backward into a hidden chute that will after a slide of astonishing duration drop you into a gnashing meat-grinder. In various other places in this room there are other trap-doors that will after slides of astonishing duration deposit you in various chambers dominated by flame-throwers, King Cobras, lasers, infuriated chimpanzees, hammers, spikes, industrial lathes, giant lampreys, belt sanders, trampolines aimed at spike ceilings, quicksand, toxic waste, high-voltage grids, a selection of poison gases and in one chamber from which I've pumped out all moisture, where you would arrive only after a slide of astonishing duration, a deep pit of salt heated by sun lamps which will over the course of several hours turn you into beef jerky. Indeed, one might say that we sit, enjoying our cake and conversation, in the most dangerous room in all the world, a place that my visitors leave with impunity only if I am satisfied that they represent no threat: a high bar that you, sir, have not yet navigated."

"I presume that I am safe as long as we remain cordial."

"And as long as I am confident that you are not wasting my time. But I have agreed, out of professional courtesy, to answer your questions. You may proceed."

"One small one, before I get into the main reason I'm here. Why must there always be a slide of astonishing duration?"

"The spatial considerations of several such rooms in close proximity. If your impregnable fortress has only one, then a mere trap door is more than sufficient; you just have to position it directly beneath a trap door. If, like some spendthrift masterminds, you want one in every room, you run into logistical difficulties that go with also placing the supporting mechanics, things like the gears that push the walls together, the vast holding tanks necessary for storing all that acid whenever it's not in use, or even the access tunnels that your minions must later navigate in order to maintain the works, or retrieve the corpses. Generally, sir, the more sophisticated the chamber, the larger its full architectural footprint, from the 3 to 1 ratio of those that employ hydraulic presses to the twenty to one ratio of those that involve the release of wildlife—and where such places are clustered beneath an anteroom like this one, the full scale of the complex can involve multiple levels in a teeming warehouse of death, where guests like yourself must traverse significant distances before arriving at the destinations that either chance or whim has chosen for them. In a facility like this one, those chutes can be as multi-branched as the plumbing in a high-rise Marriott. And I know that this is not the question that brought you here, so enough delay. Please. This is not about curiosity. This is about actual, compelling concern. How many I help you?"

Bank took a deep breath, expelled it, and shuffled forward in his seat, a coiled spring capable of covering the distance between himself and the maker of deathtraps in a single leap. If it came to that, he knew, Olgarthe would be dead in a heartbeat, and the one factor that prevented the Super-Spy from indulging himself was the awareness that he would likely be dead himself, one heartbeat after that; the room would have had to indulge its master with that many safeguards.

So he said, "Why have I always escaped?"

The pallet of emotions that made up Olgarthe's facial expressions now took another, actual pity.

"No one is ever killed," he said, "except in the room fated to kill them."

"That's no answer."

"It is your answer, my good sir. I have designed and built a room designed to utterly counter all your resourcefulness, to strike at the very base of your character, to utterly stymie all your capacities for escape. It will be a slow death, but it will be a certain one, inevitable and inexorable. Not one of your extraordinary skills can counter it, and you will be pleased to know that in the year you have spent searching for me I have provided it free to all evil organizations and ruthless masterminds with whom you could ever find yourself in direct confrontation. That includes myself. The trap door is in this room. You may not know it, sir, but you have been neutralized."

* * * *

Bank killed Olgarthe and escaped the room.

What? You want details?

The process involved a lightning-fast lunge, an unerring gunshot, a flip over the back of Olgarthe's chair, a mid-stream course correction based on no data less subtle than a barely audible click, an instantaneous calculation, and an unerring leap toward mortal danger instead of away from it. Describing the precise maneuvers would take about ten thousand words of prose; actually experiencing them took less than three seconds. Suffice it to say that when the laser beams crossed the available space, Bank was in that space but untouched; that when the darts laced with Black Mamba venom whistled through the air they disturbed not one thread of his tuxedo; that when the trap doors opened he was not trusting in the seeming solidity of those places and therefore not subjected to gravity's contribution. Perhaps only one man in twenty million could have made it five steps across that gauntlet; perhaps only one in two hundred million could have made it ten steps; and perhaps only one in two billion could have made it past what (by the time he made it through the opposite threshold), a room-sized universe of homicide, thereby dodged, evaded, wriggled past, squirmed under, and just plain defied. It was statistically impossible for anyone belonging to the teeming mass of humanity, worldwide, to get through all that to the exit corridor, and Bank managed even that, a feat of survival that had never been approached and would never be duplicated. Later, when the forensic team came to examine the videos that had captured the act from every conceivable angle, they all had to agree that the man had indeed accomplished an outright impossibility, that in the years to come would be shown to every fresh class of recruits, both to learn what role model they were being asked to emulate, and to underline that this was literally impossible. Always, forever, half the auditorium got up to leave. This showed intelligence. When the bar can't be cleared, it just can't be cleared.

Unfortunately, there remained one final trap door just where his leather shoes touched floor, at the end of all that, and it fell away at the instant when no further miracles remained possible, and so he plummeted, defiance of any kind no longer among his options.

He plummeted, the chute that took his weight steering his form at an oblique angle that he could not follow, shepherding him into a slide of truly astonishing duration, so many minutes that Bank wondered whether his end would be met at the planet's molten core; but no. Even as he thought that he had achieved terminal velocity, the chute curved upward and then in some hard-to-define alternative direction that ate up his momentum to what seemed an imminent stop. Then some burst of air jets restored his hurtling speed to something so violent that the flesh of his cheeks rippled from it, and this kept him going somewhat further until he again seemed to slow, and was artificially accelerated again.

He wondered if this was some kind of bloody metaphor for his very existence, a constant trajectory toward destruction that never arrived at that destination.

But, no: he did get to the place where Olgarthe had sent him.

● ● ● ●

This is the Super-Spy Bank, delivered at long last to the one fate he has never prepared for.

You will find him at the Warehouse Superstore. He is in the plumbing section. He wears the green apron that is part of the official franchise uniform, thick glasses that magnify his watery eyes, and a professional smile that is friendly enough but, for those who look close, a dead giveaway that he longs for escape but cannot find the necessary tools anywhere in this vast emporium that functions as shrine to drill bits and hinges. He is no longer a physical paragon and indeed has a little pot belly, that functions as the only fat part of himself, on a body that is otherwise limp and stringy. You can ask him about any kind of plumbing supply you want. He will lead you to the correct shelf, with a smile.

When his shift is over he heads to his mini-van, one of many in the vast parking lot, and drives it through mind-numbing traffic to a small house not paid for, in a neighborhood of many small houses like it, and it is possible that between parking and making his way to the front door he imagines a jazzy riff that announces his status as impossibly cool guy, possessing a talent for survival so keen that he can summon a distant orchestra to score his every movement. But he is not that guy, not anymore. He has passed through a curtain and is now a guy with a stringy grey combover and a history of twinges in the small of his back, a guy who upon accessing the house will say hello to his wife the real estate agent who has gone just a little too long with a sale, and to his kids whose grades in middle school reflect a special talent for precisely nothing. At night, there is television, and instead of martinis mixed to the most exacting standards, off-brand domestic beer.

Does he remember being the man he once was, the man whose worst possible fate has been realized here, by the villain who understood that for some, death is not actually the failure of the body? Among the crime lords and megalomaniacs who received the burned DVDs taken from various hidden cameras situated around the mere three or four locations that now dominate the life of this man who once hopped continents for his daily commute, this man who once knew ten languages and was able like a pro in all of them, there has always been rigorous debate. Maybe it's worse if he doesn't know, if all those memories of an exciting life are reduced to confusing memory-fragments, that for all he knows were instilled by jet-setting movies, watched in fragments while sleep crept on him; and maybe it's worse if he does know, if he recalls striding onto crowded casino floors and being instantly, obviously, the most exciting man there, wherever there happened to be. Perhaps it is more enjoyable to imagine all those razor-sharp instincts for survival intact, the capacity for handling every possible situation now turned to the question, Honey,

I can't cook tonight, can you please pick up a Pizza on the way home? All while those once-steely-eyes, now pale and watery, perpetually take in the contours of this deathtrap that will end only his heart attack at fifty, and search, forever, for that impossibility, a brilliant improvisation utilizing the available factors to finagle a way out.

Yes. That is probably worse.

THE REFRIGERATOR IN THE GIRLFRIEND

My girlfriend Amanda surprised me by installing a personal refrigerator in her abdomen. I didn't even know such a thing was possible. Amanda said, oh, sure, lots of people are getting them. It's the latest thing. Don't you remember Verna? I didn't remember meeting Verna. Amanda reminded me of a party we had been to. I remembered the party. She reminded me of a woman who had made a mortifying spectacle of herself there. I remembered that too. But the girl who had made the mortifying spectacle of herself was not Verna, just somebody who had been standing next to Verna.

I never ever succeeded in remembering Verna, who I know nothing about except that she had her own belly fridge before Amanda decided to get one for herself.

By that point Amanda and I had been a couple for nine months, living together for seven in a cramped little apartment we'd chosen only because it was acceptably close to the part of town worth being in. Beyond that, the place was classic micro-living. Its bathroom, a toilet and a sink and a tiny stall shower, was set off by a translucent sliding curtain instead of a proper wall. The clothes closet was not a closet but a rod stretching the length of one wall, that when laden with her hanging clothes and mine filled up half of what we laughingly called our living room. The shelf above it, stretching the same length, was our pantry and our library and our storage space and our TV stand. On the opposite wall, our bed occupied a loft hanging low over her drafting table, but not low enough below the ceiling, and while acceptable for sleeping was way too cramped for any but the most cautious sex, meaning that when we wanted to get frisky we had to cover the narrow patch of floor between clothes and loft with our comforter. Even our kitchenette was barely large enough to qualify for the -ette suffix, to the point where we sometimes called it a kitchenette-ette, and made a habit of draping plastic over the pull-down ironing board in order to have a sufficient food preparation surface on those rare occasions when we did any but the simplest cooking at home.

To do anything in the space we had, we had to shift objects around to create empty space in whatever part of the apartment we wanted to occupy, an exercise in determined organization that would have descended into chaos had either of us ever operated out of synch with the other. We used to joke that every new couple should live this way, that if we hadn't killed each other yet, like rats in some crowding experiment, we were probably meant to be together for life; but the truth was that we were young and the glorified closet we lived in was much of the time not much more to us than a place to store our bodies while unconscious, in between forays into a world that offered us more room to breathe. But there were tensions, in that there was never enough space to put anything, and bringing anything new into the house became a cause of serious protracted negotiation.

In that context, the belly fridge had major symbolic value. Whoever she got to do it had done a superlative job, making room for the soft-sided, collapsible chamber inside her without any obvious physical deformation of her anatomy. Whenever the fridge door was closed, you couldn't even see a seam, let alone feel it (and I must admit I tried, because there were plenty of reasons other than mechanical curiosity to run my hands over that flat, tanned midriff of hers). But a little depression of the switch hidden in her navel and that door swung open, revealing a sterile insulated space capable of maintaining a constant internal temperature of 37 degrees.

The space was unfortunately not large enough to accommodate a true abdominal six-pack that would have made the device a fervent exercise in the literal realization of a pun. There just wasn't enough room in Amanda, a svelte and elfin girl, for that to be possible without doing serious physiological damage. Her fridge was, however, large enough to store about half that much, in practice three aluminum cans or the equivalent in mini water bottles or sandwiches and snacks if we were up and about and didn't want to stop somewhere for provisions. And then it sealed up, becoming a secret compartment every bit as invisible as it had been when its existence was still unsuspected: a little additional personal space, inside her personal space.

I was appalled at first. I demanded to know the medical realities. She assured me that everything she'd had beneath the skin before was still there, if a little shifted about; and the side-effects would be few, among them increased farting as the only possible way to get rid of the heat buildup. Someday, she said, when we moved to a bigger place, it could be removed without leaving a scar. But until then the extra storage space would come in handy. And until then it would serve as reminder that for us there would always be enough space.

I remained skeptical until later that night, after we'd gone out and walked the streets and listened to the music coming out of the clubs and stopped by the river and watched the lights across the water for a while and went back to where things were happening and ran into some friends and talked with them for a while and come back to the space that belonged only to us. She hauled the comforter down from the loft and covered the floor with it and we made love in that tiny place between her work space and our closet space, her on top, warm as always, soft as always, the constant hum of her belly fridge somehow not at all distracting between the sounds I made and the sounds she made, even as the slyest possible look came over her face and she opened her belly long enough to touch the back of her coldest place and emerge with fingers that felt like ice against my chest. She closed the door and warmed what she had just cooled with her lips, and teased me with sly questions: do I feel cold to you, hmmm? What else do you want to keep in me, hmmm? Do you think you can keep me hot? Hmmm?

I had honestly never known myself to be the kind of man who makes love to a woman with a fridge in her belly. Up until this night I had never suspected that this was even one of my possible categories. But the climax, when it came, was historic, and as we lay together afterward I found myself aware that it was no small part to that extra added vibration inside her, that revved up to another speed as we neared the moment and the fan had to labor harder to keep the environment in the refrigerator at the same constant temperature. It was Amanda plus. And that night as we slept spooned, something we pretty much always had to do because of the tiny loft we shared, I lay awake aware of that constant whir inside her, the motor that was now as much a part of her as her heartbeat, or her breath, or the way she laughed.

· · · ·

I went crazy about Amanda within about five minutes of meeting her. She was funny, funky, unpredictable in most of the good ways and fortunately not in many of the bad ones. I was always a harder sell, not a turnoff but not an immediate starter either, and so her crazy trailed after my crazy by about two weeks, after which the two crazies sped up like comets. For a little while, until we realized we were doing serious damage to our respective wardrobes, we ripped the clothes off one another like lunatics. Then we calmed down, moved into this place, and buried ourselves in domesticity. Passion didn't ebb but it did become a harnessed force.

The addition of a fridge changed her in small endearing ways. She became a belly-shirt kind of girl, for one; long partial for black tops and distressed clothes worn in layers, even when it was so hot outside that it was impossible to understand how she remained cool under all of that, she now favored skimpier outfits that exposed skin and made access to the fridge convenient for both of us. Always outspoken, always uninhibited, she had also always nurtured a paradoxical shame over passing wind, blushing and stammering and apologizing over those occasions when she could not manage to flee somewhere out of earshot before letting fly; now that it happened about ten times as frequently as before she became almost arrogant about it, calling it the price for living with modern conveniences and explaining to total strangers that she had a fridge in her belly; see? She became less a girl who took care of snacks and soft drinks when she got to a place and more one who seized the opportunity to pull out a can of soda, raise an eyebrow, and say, with a little odorless poot, nothing like a good pop on a hot day. Once upon a time, she'd delivered hilarious riffs about the kind of people whose tattoos or piercings were the most interesting things about them. But she loved her fridge. She loved being the girl with the fridge in the girl.

We had access to a car we could borrow from time to time, and on balmy weekends liked to head out of the city to places where there were trails to hike and waterfalls to see. She packed her fridge in secret, and from time to time opened up to reveal whatever treats she had stored for us: grapes, wine, sometimes a little cake. When we didn't have the car we went to the park instead and she brought the treats that were many times more expensive if purchased on site; even more so when we went to the movies, and her belly proved the perfect way to avoid refreshment-stand prices (but only as long as we unscrewed the interior light bulb first, because if we didn't the sudden glow had a way of alerting management). Other times, when we had to travel in sketchy neighborhoods, it proved useful in ways that had nothing to do with the storage of food and drink;

it was a personal safe, keeping our valuables secure even as we pretended that we really did have nothing of value on us.

A few times we found ourselves in dark places without a flashlight and she opened up her door, revealing the light that always came on, to reveal what was now, by default, her most private place.

"I've always been bright," she said.

"You've always been cool," I replied.

We joked about the little man who lived inside her refrigerator, making sure the light turned on and off, and I affected great jealousy over his literally moving in on my girl, threatening to wring the little fucker's neck if he ever tried anything funny. We made up stories about him. I made Amanda laugh a good long time by bringing home a little fashion model doll and offering it to Amanda as a blind date for the refrigerator man. She slipped it into the fridge and much, much later, when I'd completely forgotten about it, produced the doll, its clothes ripped, its hair mussed, its feet missing one of its two detachable high-heel shoes. Amanda told me, "Look. The poor dear's been ravaged."

For a long time we hauled down the comforter even more often than we had before, driven by the new ritual Amanda had come up with: the secret post-coital snack surprise, unveiled without the need of any special exodus to the more conventional mini-fridge only a few feet away. Sometimes she made me close my eyes so I didn't know what to expect, before feeding me whatever she'd been storing inside her: cherries, grapes, jello, a gooey éclair. A couple of times it turned out to be champagne or soda so agitated by our lovemaking that it erupted on opening: a mock orgasm in and of itself, that somehow seemed a crucial part of the joke.

Then one night about four months into her life with a belly fridge Amanda asked me when I was going to get one.

We were streaming some zombie film on the tube when she popped the question with the too-casual air of a woman who'd been hoarding it for far too long. I didn't have enough context to understand what she was asking and for several seconds wondered why she was asking me if I'd be willing to get a zombie.

"No," she said, punching me in the arm. "A fridge. Or something. Make your own contribution."

I confessed that I hadn't even thought about it, not even a little bit. I had never wanted to carry a little fridge around in my belly.

She said, "Well, something else, then."

I asked her, Like what?"

She said, "Forget it."

It was the kind of "forget it" that women utter only in arguments like this one, where the man has committed some kind of irredeemable offense and the only offense even worse than that is his failure to understand what it was.

"No," I said, "tell me, seriously."

She said, "you haven't even thought about it at all up until now?"

I had to admit I hadn't. The fridge had struck me as a weird little sweet little eccentric little gesture, something that added a little welcome strangeness to lives that could always use a little welcome strangeness, but it had never occurred to me, even for a moment, to consider it the kind of romantic gesture that needed to be reciprocated. It certainly hadn't struck me as the kind of thing that she might have been waiting for: something that had turned my silence on the subject into an exercise in unmet expectations. But the look on her face revealed that this had all also been the wrong thing to say, and so I backpedaled and said, "But we can go to wherever you went, tomorrow, and see what else they have available, okay?"

She sniffed. "Don't do me any favors."

I said, "Come on, Amanda. I'm trying here."

She looked away, but by now I could tell she was in the phase of the argument where she was actively trying to remain mad, because of the power over me that it would give her for a few more minutes. She'd already gotten the concession. It was victory.

The zombie movie ended. It was a warm night so we opened the window and went out to the fire escape, and from there to the rooftop opposite our narrow alley, where we sometimes went if we didn't want to go anywhere else but where we didn't go too often because we could reach it only if we braced ourselves on the railing and then took a giant step over a gap that promised a truly fucked future if we ever slipped and fell. It was just a roof and it was better than our own, where we went rarely, only because it had one side that offered an almost unobstructed view of a neighborhood we liked; not much of a reason to court crippling injury. But tonight we bridged the abyss and crossed the pigeon-crap minefield to the overlook, and stood there for long minutes enjoying the breeze and the lights and the quiet that comes after a tiff, if this was indeed after the tiff and not some moment in relative calm in the middle of it.

She asked me if I was thirsty.

I said I was.

She opened her belly and pulled out a bottle of my favorite hard cider, so hard to find locally that we greeted the discovery of any store that carried it an occasion for genuine celebration.

I took it and said, "What about you?"

She said she wasn't thirsty.

"Are you sure? Because I can go back downstairs and get you something."

She said, "If you had a belly fridge you wouldn't have to."

I tried to think of an acceptable reply.

She said I'll take a slug of yours, and guzzled a third of the bottle. Then she handed it back. At my momentary aghast expression she grinned and bumped her hip against mine. We drew close and watched the lights for a while, saying nothing, the silence between us growing relaxed as the blowup was rescheduled.

* * * *

Life did what life does and intruded. I had two double-shifts at the steak house and she had to hit her drafting table to complete an illustration assignment that had come in with a tight deadline. The argument faded into the background and we talked about other things, heading downtown on the third night to be with friends, including the friend of a friend who had had a church key imbedded on one palm and a can opener imbedded on the other. Everybody complimented him. I said it must make jerking off difficult. He said, yeah, I get that a lot. The conversational possibilities of this were now exhausted, but then some latecomers joined us and the guy ended up showing off his church key and can opener a second time. Then an hour later some new folks came around and he brought them up to date with iteration number three. I noted out loud that the chief drawback of imbedded equipment like that seemed to be the necessity of explaining it. Folks who just carried a church key on their key ring didn't have to point it out to everybody who passed within earshot. The guy grinned and said, really.

Later, as we made our way home, Amanda said, "Why do you have to be like that?"

I said, "Be like what?"

"The way you were with whatsisname."

"He didn't seem to mind it."

"He said he gets that a lot. Which isn't the same thing."

"What do you expect me to say? That I'm impressed? Because I wasn't. It was one of the fucking lamest things I've ever seen."

She said, "Like my fridge."

"That's different."

"How?"

"Well, in the first place, it's different because I love you. I loved you before you had your fridge and I had a lot of things to love about you before you had your fridge. I want to be with you because I already see you as a lot more than a fridge with legs. This schmuck, whose name I notice you can't remember either, I know absolutely nothing about except that he once thought it vitally important that for as long as he lived he'd never again have any trouble opening cans of baked beans. It's one stupid trick and it's lame. Why would I be impressed?"

We walked in silence for a while, and I was just foolish enough to think I'd won the argument. She had time to pass wind twice.

Then she asked me, "Do you think my fridge is lame?"

I said, "I think your fridge is great, but it's not the part of you I care about most, no."

"I got it for us."

"I know, I appreciate that. I thought it was sweet as hell. But even so, we don't live in the goddamned Taj Mahal. I'm never more than three steps from the mini-fridge the place came with. I can walk those three steps. It's not something our entire relationship needs to rest on, you know? Seriously, what are we even talking about?"

We walked a little further. It was a clear night in the middle of summer but a cold front had rolled in and in just a few minutes the temperature had lowered from cool and comfortable to cool and not quite warm enough for the way we were dressed; a blast of air we didn't expect hit us as we emerged from the wind-break of some storefronts to the open space of the busiest intersection between us and home. It wasn't freezing or anything, but it made home and bed someplace I wanted to get sooner rather than later. The lights were with us but turning, so we had to hurry across the street in order to make it before traffic cut us off, and what with one thing or another we were halfway to the next intersection before Amanda said, "You don't really want to get one for yourself, do you?"

I wanted to snap no. Instead I told her I would go with her to whoever did hers as soon as we could make our way there and see the possibilities. Just no can openers. They were stupid.

She said okay.

We got home. It wasn't all that late but we were tired and stressed out and not in the mood for anything more than going to bed. The comforter didn't get hauled down. I got undressed and climbed up into the loft, scooting all the way against the wall so she'd have room to join me when she got around to following. She said she wasn't quite ready for bed yet and would work a little at her table before coming in after me. She asked me if that was okay. I said sure it was okay. The lamp came on, and the glow spilled upward from around the edges of the loft, like the first rays of a sunrise making itself known before it gets around to rising in the East. I wanted to call her up and say all the important things, among them that I didn't like the way our grip on one another seemed to be loosening, all of a sudden. But I didn't. Instead I just curled up in the shadow of her light and listened to the scratching of her pencil against the card stock. I closed my eyes, fell asleep, dreamed, and much later, woke again, to that same occluded light and the same sound of Amanda, still working, near me but not anywhere I could see.

* * * *

We went to the same guy who installed her fridge, whose establishment was two flights of stairs above a night club we'd visited once and despised, for more reasons than I need to get into because we hadn't been there since. The stairs began at the vestibule to the club and rose past the ambience we'd hated to another I found not much of an improvement: a narrow hallway illuminated by one wedge of light at the far end.

The first thing we saw when we entered the parlor was a woman with raccoon eyes lying naked on a bench while a man fried link sausages on her bare belly. The heated portion of her anatomy was marked by a glowing red circle and the flashing letters WARNING: STOVE IS HOT. Her boyfriend or product tester or whatever the hell he was turned the links with a spatula, to ensure even cooking. Her hot spot was so shiny from the sausages that I couldn't help wondering why her boyfriend or whatever didn't use a frying pan, but that would have been too stupid a question to ask out loud. Nothing stopped him from using a frying pan. Cooking on her bare skin was the whole point.

Amanda asked her if it hurt.

The woman said, "Naaah, it's all insulated."

I said, "Yeah, but what about grease spatter? I get spot burns all the time, just standing at a hot stove."

She gave me the kind of look reserved for people who crap their pants on purpose. Naaah, she said, we thought of that. She pressed the lit end of her cigarette against her right nipple, to no ill effect, and explained: "See? I'm insulated all over." Then she went back to studying the ceiling with the bored patience of a home inspector looking for roof leaks.

The curtains in the back of the room parted and the proprietor came out, looking about what I'd expected him to look like, best described as a guy once caught in a shrapnel explosion who had decided he liked his face with all the little metal bits still stuck in his skin wherever they hit. He would have been bald, I guess, but he'd also implanted silver fiber optic hair glowing pink at the tips. He said yo to Amanda and she said yo to him and he asked her how her fridge was working and she said it was great and he looked at me and said, "So what are you in the market for?"

I said I wasn't in the market for anything in particular but was willing to hear suggestions. So we went into the back room to talk about the possibilities and I got my education in just how far the tech had come. Nothing really grabbed me. I didn't want to turn my butt cheeks into a microwave or my dick into a power-vac or my kidney into a blender, because none of that had ever intersected with my fantasies in any way. But this had become some kind of weird relationship power struggle I didn't understand and I knew that if I backed down now the sudden strange friction between Amanda would me would certainly escalate. So I gave an unenthusiastic yes to the toaster oven. Amanda interjected that a pop-up toaster would be even cooler, but I thought a couple of parallel slit orifices in my abdomen would be a bit much. A toaster oven that could be hidden under flesh like Amanda's fridge, something that I could pretend wasn't there most of the time, that would be fine. So I said, naaah, make it the toaster oven. We can do a lot more than just make toast, with a toaster oven.

He said, "That takes a few hours to install. We'll have to make an appointment for that one." Consulting his ledger, he said, "Noon Saturday okay?"

I said fine. Any number of things could happen between now and Saturday.

But I wasn't going to get out of there that easily. Amanda grew petulant and asked him if there was something small I could do today so I didn't go away empty-handed.

"Oh, sure," said the guy.

And so, over the next twenty minutes, he put in my reading lamp.

The procedure wasn't very invasive, nothing compared to what Amanda had put herself through. It was just a thin light-emitting strip imbedded in my chin, just beneath the skin. You couldn't see it when it was off. But if I needed the lamp I could click the activator with my tongue and the light would come on. It was light with the same reddish tint you get when you try to cover a flashlight with your fingers, but it was bright enough to read by, and a likely life-saver in situations where it was dark and I was had having trouble fitting a key into a lock. I supposed it was not a bad thing to have. Amanda told me it was beautiful and asked me if I liked it. I didn't tell her that when I went to the bathroom, turned off the lights, and flicked my chin light on to see what it looked like in the mirror, I was a little disturbed by the spooky effect the blood-tinged lighting from below had on my face, what with the streaks of scarlet along my jaw and cheekbones making me look like I'd just been face-down in viscera. It would be useful on Halloween, I supposed. But I left the bathroom with a smile on my face and told Amanda it was great.

* * * *

We stayed out late and returned home to a dark apartment, where we had some of the best sex in our shared history. Amanda pulled down the comforter and said, let's fuck with the light on. She didn't mean any of our lamps, which wouldn't have been unusual, but mine. I said why not. So we turned off all other ambient sources of light, even pulling down the blackout shade so we couldn't get any neon or moonlight or light sources opposing apartment windows filtering in on us from the alley. I turned on my chin and she said oooh, look at him, and I said whatever stupid rejoinder came to mind and we got into it, missionary style, our proximity caging the red brilliance between us and making tiny scarlet flames dance in her eyes. We finished up, I rolled off and she immediately climbed on, insatiable, saying that this time she wanted the spotlight. With her energetic help I recovered faster than I ever had and we went a second time, slower, her riding me, lit from below, my chin casting a distorted but still recognizable silhouette of her on the ceiling.

Afterward, she rolled off and we lay side by side, facing the pink tint of the ceiling. The spotlight may have been dimmer, at that remove, than it had been within coital range, but I saw no reason to turn my chin off. It wasn't a bad afterglow to have.

I said, "Whoo."

"Yeah," she said. "Whoo."

"Got a snack?"

"You're gonna have to go to the kitchen. I'm not stocked."

"Really?"

"Of course really. It's not automatic, you know. There's not always going to be something there. I have to put something in, in order to have something to take out."

"I'm just saying. You usually."

"Well today, I forgot. It's no big deal."

"Okay, okay."

I got up and went to the kitchenette-ette, popping open the fridge and finding only one half-consumed bottle of water there. It was that or crap from the tap. Our building had tinny crap from the tap. So I took the water bottle and brought it back to the comforter and took a sip, handing the rest of the bottle to Amanda.

I said, "Did you like it with the light?"

She drained the bottle. "What do you think?"

"I think it was great."

"Me too. Never better."

"I love you."

"Me, too."

But hers sounded no better than polite.

It had been as good as we ever got but as soon as it was over everything that had been bothering her had bubbled back to the surface, as if to prove that we hadn't been able to drown it. "What's wrong?"

"Nothing."

Again, daring me to figure it out.

This was not the best time for me to say one of those stupid boyfriend things that comes out of a man's mouth already feeling like a mistake and enters the room with all the grace of a three-year-old running naked into a fancy dinner party and shouting, "doodie!" Even as I heard myself speak my next words I wanted to reach after them with both hands, yank them out of the air and stuff them back down my throat.

I said, "I seriously don't think it would have been all that much better if I'd been able to make you some toast now."

The way her eyes turned toward me, right then, should have provided me with sufficient warning to shut up.

She said, "What."

"I'm just saying. I know you're disappointed I didn't get my toaster oven today. But it wouldn't have made that much of a difference, right? I mean, you can't tell me that the number one thing on your mind right now is toast."

"You never know. Maybe I used up so many carbs getting you off twice I want to pound down half a loaf of cinnamon raisin right now."

"I'm just saying."

"You sure expected your stupid snack."

I blew up. "Damn straight I expected the snack. I don't need the snack, I don't require the snack, I don't get mad at you when you don't have the snack, but for God's sake I saw nothing wrong in asking for the snack, because every time we've made love since you got that damned fridge you've always offered me a snack. You trained me to expect it, so I asked. It's Pavlovian."

"You're right. You're absolutely right. I shouldn't ever offer you a beer unless I intend to always have a beer ready. In fact, while I'm at it I'll have to flatten the top of my head so you'll always have a place to put it down."

Having this hoary chestnut of arrogant prick humor shoved in my face didn't do anything but piss me off. "You'd make a terrible coffee table."

"Why?

"You're too goddamned tall."

It would have been hard to say, in the next four seconds, whether it was her eyes or her mouth that described the best circles. Either way, I knew that I had taken it one step too far. She got up and drew aside the hanging curtain that separated the bathroom from the rest of the room, pulling it back into place behind her. In our apartment this was the equivalent of a slammed door, sealing her behind what the unspoken rules of etiquette in our relationship dictated that I respect as solid walls. It was stupid, but it wasn't a fiction I felt like shattering right now, so I grumbled and muttered to myself and gathered up the comforter to return it to its non-coital location on the loft. Meanwhile, she started running the shower: another layer of separation.

I turned on the apartment lights so I could switch off my chin.

• • • •

We cancelled the Saturday appointment. I volunteered for extra shifts so I wouldn't have to go home. When I did get home she was either absent or already asleep. When she was home she was so sullen I made no overtures. We spoke only to negotiate the minutiae of apartment living, confirming whether or not the garbage had indeed been taken out, the front door indeed locked, the toilet indeed flushed. I ate out or brought food in from outside to spare myself the uncomfortable prospect of taking anything from the fridge in the kitchenette-ette, a wholly innocent use of an innocent appliance that in context now suddenly seemed like further provocation. When I found her awake and working, I climbed to the loft first and put her in the position of deciding whether or not to climb in after me. When I found her already up there, I hauled out our extra comforter and slept on the floor instead.

For at least four nights the question seemed not if we were going to break up but when.

That surprisingly didn't happen. The chill thawed, but not because of any grudging apologies, rather because maintaining a fight on that scale requires a lot of conscious effort and neither one of us was up to it. Sooner or later, one of us forgot we were supposed to be fighting and said something civil. The other forgot to reject it. Then the other one said something affable and again received no angry retaliation. From there it moved on to friendly and from there to affectionate. We exchanged smiles. We did little favors for one another. Eventually, we kissed again; not long after that, we made love again, me not using my reading lamp, her not offering me another treat from her fridge, our respective modifications becoming attributes unused and un-remarked, baggage that neither one of us wanted to bring up. The big question was now not whether we'd always have the remaining tension between us but how and when it would manifest again.

Then one night we went to a party to catch up with friends, and found that a large number of them had new appliances to show off. One guy had turned his arm into a scrolling message board and for the better part of an hour took suggestions over what text to program into it, an exercise that inevitably grew dull as it devolved into a competition over who could come up with the most offensive suggestions. One woman dispensed frozen daiquiris from her nipples, strawberry from the left and coconut from the right. Somebody we didn't know who might have been kidding offered to cook waffles on his butt. It came around to Amanda and me, and requests for her to show off her fridge and me to show off my reading lamp. Amanda said she wasn't dressed for it, and I noticed for the first time that she hadn't dressed in one of her midriff-baring outfits for easy access. I said that my lamp was on the fritz and that I wouldn't be able to turn it on again until I went in for repairs.

Then another couple we knew said that they had the best modifications ever. He rolled up his shirt and pulled out a baby bottle, kept warm by body heat. She rolled up hers and revealed something she'd gotten to go along with the beginnings of a baby bump: a belly pouch, to carry the little one around after in infancy. "I'm a marsupial," she beamed. The crowd showered them with congratulations.

Not long afterward Amanda whispered in my ear that she had to get the hell out of there before she exploded. We made our excuses and left.

It was a cool but comfortable weekend night and so we drifted in the direction of the river. The sidewalks teemed with happy and laughing people. We walked in silence among them, pausing here and there to look in a shop window or to make way for larger groups. We stopped for a long time at a bridge overlooking the water, watching the party boats go by and saying nothing of any real consequence until Amanda said, "It's really all pretty much ridiculously beside the point, isn't it?"

I exhaled in relief. "Yeah. It is. It really, really is."

We kissed, earning a light cheer from tourists in a sightseeing boat, just before they disappeared under the bridge. I told her I loved her and she said she loved me and we kissed again, this time not earning a cheer because the boat had passed and there were no others in range.

She rested her forehead on mine. "I almost had it removed, the other day. The fridge, I mean."

"I never wanted you to do that."

"I know. But I almost did. I passed by the shop and considered dropping in to make arrangements. But then I thought, why should I? It's not hurting anything, where it is. I can still make good use of it, sometimes. It just doesn't have to be the center of anything. That makes sense, right?"

"Perfect sense. But while we're on the subject, I passed by the shop too."

"Oh, no. Don't tell me you got the toaster oven!"

"I've got to admit, it was a near thing. I wanted to do something, to get past whatever the hell's been going on with us. But the more I thought about it, the stupider it seemed. Nobody needs that much goddamned toast in his life. And I knew I didn't want to carry around the same thing we were fighting about. But while I was there I did stop in and confirm that there was something else I could get installed, something a lot simpler and more important than a toaster, that I could save for a rainy day."

"What?"

"I don't have it yet. Like I said, it was just something I considered. But I think I'll surprise you with it, someday soon."

"You're such a tease."

"The worst," I confirmed.

We kissed again and went downstairs to the river level, site of a gourmet coffee shoppe we frequented a lot less than we would have liked. She saved one of the waterfront tables and I went to the counter, returning a few minutes later with lattes and a pair of the establishment's jumbo cupcakes, the kind of snack that could make a starving person fat just by looking at it.

Amanda had never been a calorie-counter. She'd never needed to be. But the party we'd left had already included a buffet with a selection of comfort foods and desserts that neither one us had denied ourselves. So she regarded the unexpected treat, a pink monstrosity that all by itself probably met a full week's minimum required carb count, with a palpable mixture of longing and dismay, her mind racing through the hundred and one mental negotiations that would permit her to allow the additional indulgence. After a minute or so, the inner treaty with her conscience was both signed and notarized. "We can split one. I'll store the other away for another night."

I shook my head and took her by the wrist before she could pull up her shirt.

To her round and startled eyes I said, "Please not the fridge. This one I'd like to be for right now."

Her smile was blinding. "Okay."

So she inhaled half of it in one bite, getting the required amount of pink cream on her nose.

THE SECRET AMBASSADOR

Early that morning five heavily-armed and physically intimidating men had burst into my Florida home, cuffed me, dragged me out with a bag over my head and hauled me off to the nearest Air Force base, where I was loaded aboard a plane to parts unknown.

At this point it would be amusing to say that this was only the third time this had ever happened to me, but no: it was the first.

Once I was on the plane, they removed my handcuffs and took the bag off my head. It was a private jet, very clean and elegant. The only other apparent occupants were three very large and formidable-looking men who didn't pay me much mind but who wore the demeanor of guys who would have been than amenable to dislocating all my joints if I showed enough bad judgment to misbehave in any way. I chose to remain in my seat. An attendant came by to offer me my choice of complimentary beverage. As a small act of rebellion, I named an obscure regional soda that I had loved in my childhood and that I had long considered defunct until just last year discovering a six-pack in a rustic general store that I happened to stumble across, without warning. She brought me the obscure regional soda. "We've researched you," she explained. Then she asked me if I wanted any ice. I said that sure, ice would be fine. I drank my soda without really tasting it, and the jet headed northwest, stopped after many hours to refuel, and then took off again. I asked for permission to go to the bathroom and was told that I did not have to ask, that I should not be silly, and that I was not among barbarians. I went to the bathroom, considered some *Die Hard* scenario in which I disappeared into cargo storage and came out only to eliminate my hulking captors one at a time before finally seizing control of the cockpit, but could think of about a thousand reasons why this wouldn't have been a good idea, and so returned to my seat, where a fresh can of that favored soda was waiting.

After many hours in the air a woman I had never seen before emerged from the curtain in the rear of the passenger cabin. She had silvery hair even though her features seemed too smooth for her to aged into it naturally, and she wore it in a beehive of the sort I had often privately called a probable nesting place for bats. Bifocals dangled from a chain around her neck. Her smile was sweet and non-threatening, though I like most people had experienced exactly that smile on the faces of women who looked like this, in whose mouths butter would have refused to melt. It was the kind of charm one experiences from people who don't really possess any charm: a "you are screwed and I am more than happy to tell you about it" kind of smile. Or maybe not; maybe it was a warm smile and I was just projecting.

She sat in one of the other seats and that is how I discovered that they were designed to pivot, allowing her to face me.

She said, "Are you having a comfortable flight?"

I blinked. It had sounded like she'd asked me if I was having a comfortable flight.

"Aside from being on a plane I did not wake up this morning expecting to board, and not knowing why, sure." And then, because the situation called for additional awkwardness, I found myself babbling: "You had my soda."

"Yes, well. You may take that as evidence that our intentions toward you are mostly benign."

I seized on the most troublesome word. "Mostly."

"I am committed to being honest with you, sir."

In movies the guy abducted by a mysterious but clearly well-connected conspiracy has all the relevant questions stored up in a mental database and can rattle them off at will and in the proper order without ever steering the exposition into unprofitable avenues. Movies have to be like that because they are of finite length and it is therefore more helpful to the story to get past all of the necessary explanations in as short a slice of the running time as possible. Me, I didn't know what to ask next, and so I immediately lowered my attention to my soda, which was down to the dregs, the straw making the kind of exhausted sound straws make when the source runs dry. The same attendant whose only job appeared to be keeping me supplied ran out, put down a fresh can, and once again disappeared behind the curtain, making me think the insane thought that she might have been going back there to assist Oz.

Beehive flashed teeth. "I know this must be confusing, but it's all very simple. The President of the United States has appointed you the Secret Ambassador to Alaska."

I expected her to continue, but it seemed that no further words would be forthcoming unless I solicited them. "This raises more questions than it answers."

"I expect it would."

"Among them," I said, "the simple objection that Alaska is part of the United States and that no country ever sends ambassadors to itself."

"You would think so," she said, with perfect manufactured empathy. "But the history is complicated. The post was established back when Alaska was only a United States possession, and was considered sufficiently useful that it's never been eliminated. The law requires somebody."

"And you couldn't just appoint somebody from the State Department?"

"There are long and complicated reasons why this wouldn't work. Later, I may issue you a pamphlet that will provide you with all the necessary history, along with some colorful anecdotes about figures who were instrumental in forging your current predicament, among them the Presidents Roosevelt (Teddy), Taft, and Harding. The Taft story is particularly amusing. But you may familiarize yourself with this material at your leisure, as you will have more than enough opportunity to do so. In the meantime, this is the situation. You have been selected by an unassailable algorithm to serve a grateful nation as the Secret Ambassador to Alaska, and must obey."

Nothing I had heard yet made any sense. "I have no background in diplomacy."

"Alaska is part of the United States and you won't need any."

"I'm socially awkward and likely to cause an international incident. Or whatever gets caused when a guy breaks protocol in an embassy to his own country."

"There will be no official functions of the sort you imagine. You will only be Ambassador for a few days."

"That seems intensely pointless."

"It does, but it is enshrined in law and we must respect it."

"Why did you have to take me against my will?"

She said, "As stated, this is very complicated."

"I'm not fit for cold weather. I get bronchial. That's why I live in Florida."

That smile flickered again. It had pink spots from her lipstick, and in my current state of mind it was hard to not regard that as blood. "The temperature at the embassy is now a balmy sixty degrees, Fahrenheit. You might need a jacket at night, but only if you step out onto the deck, to stand beneath the unspoiled sky and enjoy the most spectacular starscape that you, as accustomed as you are to the light-pollution problems of the more populated places you have always inhabited. it will only be for one night. We will provide the mosquito repellent. It will all be very pleasant."

I suspected already that it would not be; perhaps something in the way that sweet smile of hers never touched her eyes. It was toxic sweetness, and it was like my fate was being directed by everyone's worst distant aunt. I said, "Anything else?"

"This will be your complete itinerary. You will arrive at 11 AM local time at a small airfield near the coast, where you will be escorted to a limousine Humvee with security motorcade two hundred and forty miles to an isolated and little-visited national park where rolling hills surround a peaceful lake of extraordinary natural beauty. Snow-capped mountains, bridged by glaciers, will be visible in the distance, but where you are it will only be cold enough to require a fleece. From there you will be taken to the Embassy, a lodge equipped with sauna, library, exercise room and a fine selection of cheeses. You will be able to spend your evening any way you like, with professional companions if you desire. In the morning, following a sumptuous continental breakfast, a judge will arrive to swear you in, at which point the Federal Government will direct deposit twenty million dollars into your savings account."

That part didn't suck. "Um."

"At that point the motorcade will return you to the airport, where you will be flown via jet and helicopter to various other locations around the State, some quite lovely, and some quite isolated, a few of them villages accessible only by air. At each location, you will make speeches that have been written for you, none of them too long or too burdened by native pronunciations."

I said, "That doesn't sound very Secret."

"There's a limit to how Secret you can be. People will know that you're an important government official there to brief them on local land rights, or fishing quotas, or something. In one case you will be cutting the ribbon at the dedication of a new high school, named after a Police Chief who last year drowned in two inches of water under unfortunate and demeaning circumstances. The one thing they will not know is that you are Ambassador. That's where the secret comes in. For these reasons you will depart without taking any questions. You are never to depart from the script. Is that clear?"

"I reserve judgment."

"On the fifth day you will be treated by a banquet by various dignitaries, who are in on the secret and will openly thank you for everything you have done for this country. On the sixth you will be taken by another jeep to another remote location where you will have an arranged encounter with an polar bear."

I had been a devotee of managed wildlife encounters, and had enjoyed several in my life, including one with a manatee, one with a friendly dolphin, and one with a puma. I'd even petted a tiger, once. The thought of visiting a polar bear made me gulp. "Is that even safe?"

Here came that bloody smile again. "In the sense that the danger will be kept within the expected parameters, yes. This will not be a juvenile or tamed animal. This is a magnificent adult polar bear, well-fed by its keepers, ten feet tall when standing on its hind legs, and well-used to encounters with ambassadors from the lower 48. If it were wild, it would likely disembowel you and then take its time feasting on your still-living form. But it knows how to behave. It won't eat you."

"Are you sure?"

"I am sure. I have attended this annual ritual with seventeen Ambassadors before you. The polar bear always respected the script and its obligation, if it wanted a steady diet of seals, to do exactly what we expected from it. What will happen is that it will wait for its cue, the singing of the National Anthem, then approach you making all the threat-displays normally to be expected by a predator of the sort. It will place its paws, which are quite large, on your shoulders. It will lower its giant head until you are nose to nose, and it will, I believe the word is, 'boop' you. I have been told that the psychological effect on an ambassador is magical and humbling. It's very cute. You will feel one with nature. And then, it will dig its claws into your flesh and rip off both your arms."

"What?"

"Again, the polar bear has been trained. It will hook its claws into your specific junction of shoulder and arm, and cleanly tear your arms from their sockets. It will not eat the arms. It will not do you any further damage. It will understand that its duty is done, and it will waddle off happy to surrender itself to the custody of keepers who have a nice seal for it to enjoy. There is no chance of it remaining by your side, to enjoy the more convenient meal. To a polar bear, a seal is the perfect meal. A human being tastes bad. This polar bear has had both and knows the difference, including critically the lesson that doing any further harm to you means that it won't get the seal. You will, aside from the amputation of your arms, be perfectly fine."

"But, I'll be lying there with no arms, bleeding out!"

"Initially, yes. But you will not bleed out. You will be immediately tended by a squad of paramedics. They will stabilize you and fly both you and your arms to a hospital that will re-attach them. The team is very experienced at this procedure and has never lost an ambassador. Not all of you regain the full function of your arms, and most retain a level of paralysis in the hands, as well as lifelong pain issues, but everybody lives through it, and all leave Alaska with a fortune in the bank, a non-disclosure agreement and whatever assistance they might need, moving forward."

I opened my mouth, closed it, opened it again, made little circles with my hand that completely duplicated the internal process via which I was struggling to find speech, said something that sounded like Guh, and then glanced at the two bored security behemoths near the cockpit, who regarded me with both bored indifference and the unspoken message that if I rose and started punching things, they would be more than happy to respond with blows of their own. I almost lost control of my bowels. I almost started screaming. But the cold hands of sanity grasped me by my still-intact shoulders and forced me to remain in my seat, where I finally regained control. "Why?"

Here I saw her betray the first stirrings of empathy.

"In government," Beehive said, "certain policies that seemed like a good idea at the idea re maintained long after their rationale is forgotten. Our predecessors said that this was important, and they were sufficiently vehement about it that they are still not questioned, even though the original impetus has been lost. For what it's worth, you will have the undying gratitude of the Secretaries of State and the Interior."

"And this . . . just happens?" I managed.

"It's a genuine American tradition," she replied.

"And you expect me to be quiet about it forever?"

"Not forever," she said, providing me with yet another glimpse of those stained teeth. They were not, actually, bad teeth; not what it now seemed like they should be, fangs. They were just teeth, of the sort that could have been found on a school crossing guard, or a librarian. I realized, with the worst horror I'd felt yet, that she was not actually feigning warmth. Butter would have melted in her mouth after all. Despite everything, she liked me. "Because once you are retired from your service in Alaska, you will go on to your next posting, as the Secret Ambassador to North Dakota."

She dabbed at her mouth with a paper napkin.

"And, unfortunately, nobody's ever lived through that."

A DEARTH OF DRAGONS

Partyka found me by the rock by the edge of the Great Nothing.

It wasn't all that brilliant a guess for him, that I'd be there. Few people spent much time on that side of the island, which is steep and densely wooded and not much good for anything to the folk of the village except as a windbreak, blunting the storms that roll in from the sea. I may have been the only one who bothered with the difficult climb to the overlook at the island's highest point. When I didn't have responsibilities that made me easy to find around home, and in particular around the island general store run by my father, the rock was pretty much where Partyka could always find me.

The village we called Worldview, settled centuries prior by pilgrims who must have had some persuasive reason to abandon the continent that had everything any human or almost-human could possibly want, sits on the side of the island facing all of human civilization. From that place, even on foggy days, the rocky tip of the great landmass looms on the horizon like a giant waiting for somebody to nudge him out of a sound sleep. On clear days it's possible to make out the settlements atop those distant cliffs, which mark the beginning of the world where almost everybody, except for the two hundred or so of us huddled on this stupid island, live. On clear nights, the same view offers distant lights, the handful of homes that hug the cliffs, the larger mass of the prison that sits tucked into a cleft in the walls. It is visual evidence that our own tiny speck of land is not all there was to the world. (Also, a reminder that the convicts, worst of the worst by society's measurement, are sent to the edge of the civilized world to be punished, and that we were sent here to be born; thanks a lot, God.)

There's nothing unusual about young people chafing at the confines of the island. Most of the kids I grew up with ached to cross the reach and travel across the great continent, seeing all there was to see, or at least seeing more than the same clump of houses, the same fleet of fishing boats, the same green hills and the same looming mainland cliffs. Many grow up to do that just that. That is, after all, one of the things that keeps our population small. But something was wrong with me. I was drawn in in another direction, the churning sea. I sat on the slab of flat rock that hung only half-supported over the drop of three hundred hands and watched the waters, thinking of all the mad explorers who had traveled out into that nothingness searching for frontiers, and returned—on those few occasions that they did return—with the intelligence that there weren't any. I had always wanted to travel in that direction, to find the hidden kingdoms and distant treasures that no one has ever seen, that all mapmakers tell us don't exist; the genuinely unknown places that have been so short in supply since the map we know was drawn. I wanted to be the one to plant flags and the last time anybody had been able to do that was an era centuries past, in history books.

Today that pull was worse than usual, and so it was a good thing that Partyka, who was fair and pale-eyed and lanky and possessed of a crooked grin that precisely countered his habit of holding his head at a slight tilt, came just in time to pull me out of a black mood. It was a warm day, and the hike that had taken up half his morning had turned his forehead shiny under his sandy-brown bangs. Knowing him, he'd run much of the distance, looking forward to seeing me, grinning when he spotted me on the rock and knew that he'd guessed right.

It irritated me to be known so well, even by this boy who everybody agreed I would likely marry in a year or so, when we were both seventeen and old enough. "Did you come all this way just looking for me?"

"Can you think of any better reason I should drag myself up that trail to nowhere?"

The wind whipped the hair around my face. "I like the view."

"I know. I'm not much for views unless there are pretty girls in them."

"Sit with me, then."

He didn't take a spot by my side, as he might have had he found me anywhere else. He had always called the jutting rock on which I sat a disaster waiting to happen. Rocks slide, he said. This one, eternal as it was, as marked by the boots of previous generations of young men and women as it was, only had to slide forward twice the length of a man's body before it would decide to roll, and plummet down to base of the cliff, where any riders would have been dead long before the thunderous incoming waves would have time to drown them. "You could come with me, and walk where it's safe."

"I'm safe here."

"When you stand, you can slip; and when you slip, the wind can take you, and when the wind takes you, you can die. That's a lot to pay for a view of nothing."

Partyka was more to my liking that any of the boys or girls I had grown up with—a silly, provincial lot, many of them, proud of knowing nothing, dreaming of other places but suited for life on a speck of land as tiny and as a clod of dirt of someone's boot—but sometimes his relative lack of imagination irritated me. "I don't see it as nothing."

"Say I'm a blind coward, if you must. Will you come back in, just so I can feel better?"

I stood, the wind blowing my long patched skirt against my legs like a sail battered tight against ship rigging, and for a moment imagined that wind taking hold of me, lifting me into the sky, carrying me past the great emptiness to the exotic places that I had always suspected hidden behind that endless expanse of water: a place that might offer adventure and might offer hardship but would, at bare minimum, offer *difference*. Even dragons. The stories told of dragons at the edge of the world, but as my life went on I grew more and more afraid that there were none, and further, nothing that matched them for wonder.

I hopped down on the correct side of the rock and kissed this good boy whose only real problem with me was my strangeness.

Then he stunned me. "When we're married, I'll have to give thought to building our home up here."

"A house? On this side of the island? You'd never live up here. Not if you had to look at the Nothing all day."

"I would have more to look at, all day, than the Nothing. I'd have you."

"You would have to climb down to the village and back, every day, just to work. You'll have to haul all our goods up the path."

"I'm strong," he said. "As long as we're not right up against the edge, and I don't have to worry about the whole house toppling over in my sleep, I'll be fine. You'll be worth the climb."

I thought the same things I always thought: that he was a good boy, kind and true and beautiful in his dull way, meriting much better than a girl who could not stand the world as it was; a girl who all the others around them considered peculiar at best and mad at worst. "You deserve better than me."

"Not at all. If I found some other girl, who would tell me stories?"

* * * *

That's another thing I'm considered strange for. The stories.

There are cities on the continent with great libraries and universities, containing so many shelves and histories and adventures and tales of imagination that no one lifetime would ever be enough to read them all, but here on the ocean's only island the people are not inclined to that sort of the thing, and the one library we have tops out at fifty volumes of fiction. That's a scandal. Fifty books, or one fourth of a book per person. I had them all read by the time I was twelve. I have some more myself, the accumulation of a lifetime, ordered through our regular supply drops, but fifty for a town?

I once made the mistake of complaining about this to a boy I knew, not Partyka but another, square-faced and broad-chested Reglan, who responded the way I fear too many of his neighbors would: "So? What's the use of stories? They're not real. They're just things to fool yourself with, if you can't handle the life around you." Any hope Reglan might have had of becoming my promised had died in that moment. But he spoke for the majority of us. One day in a self-pitying mood I went to that shelf of books with a basket of leaves and placed one in the midpoint of each volume, to see if I was only one who read. A month later most of the leaves had not been disturbed. Some may be there still.

It's that lack of interest that I've ever been able to understand.

There are other islands in the world. The one continent has lakes and rivers and those are broken apart by specks of land, here and there, some with people on them and some of them with things stranger than people on them. There's plenty of room for adventurous things to happen. My mother, also a storyteller by inclination—who says she actually did write a book, once, which she says saw print between covers, though I've never seen a copy—raised me on tales of intrigue of adventure on the great continent, of kings deposed and monsters faced, of the wars between the slope-browed men of the tropics and the slant-eyed men of the northern climes; of the ships that never ventured farther than three days' sail from the great ports of the world, that only ventured that far from land to avoid shallows, but kept returning to leap-frog from one port city to another. If I told stories about such things, I would not be considered so strange. But the stories I like, both to read and to tell, claim more exists behind the sea, hidden by clouds and other veils, hiding lost kingdoms and great deeds in distant places that have somehow never been mapped. I set them in lands where men have three legs and horses speak; lands that contained treasures greater than all the wealth known to the continent, and lands where men have constructed wings capable of flying them to the moon. They make my world seem larger.

But Partyka is the only one who seems to enjoy them.

"What he saw was an unimaginable crystal city, surrounded on all sides by impenetrable forest. No man had ever seen such a glorious place, or even pictured it. But as he walked through the streets, seeing the sunlight glitter on the jeweled walls, he could not find any entrances to any of the buildings; he heard laughter, and the play of children, but no voices welcoming him in, no crowds who might guide him to shelter."

"It's a cemetery."

I hated his occasional attempts to guess a story's central idea ahead of the telling, but as it happened, on this occasion he was uncomfortably close to the revelation I'd planned. "What would make you say that?"

"Nobody's going to build a city anywhere if there's no way to get it and out of the buildings so people can use it. But if the structures are burial monuments of some kind, like the obelisks at Pyanietham, it only makes sense for the corpses inside them to be sealed in."

"And the laughter of the children?"

"I was with you when the man from the boat showed us that colorful bird from the interior, the one that could imitate sounds. He commanded it to sing, and it sounded like a choir, not just one voice, but four singing in harmony. What if there were birds like this around the city your explorer found? And what if they had once known a place where children were playing? The silly mindless things could nest in the high places and make your poor fool of traveler think that wherever he went, a mob of children was always around the next corner."

This was close enough to the twist I had planned. "I'm very upset at you."

"I've been waiting for you to tell a story based on that bird since we saw it."

"You should be nicer to me."

A mock chase followed, with laughter at the end of it; followed by a breathless kiss.

* * * *

We could have headed straight down the trail. But it was early afternoon and we had time to spend, and instead we decided to take the long way around, following the shoreline from the high points overlooking the water to the low ones that kiss it. The South and East are where the shoreline rises most gently from the water. One of the lesser streams from the wooded country joins with the ocean at the island's southernmost tip, at a little bay with fine brown sand at both banks—a site that many people would consider beautiful, but that my neighbors consider useless because there's a more useful harbor, exiting into less dangerous currents, at Worldview.

When we passed that spot and crossed the shallow stream there on the stepping stones that nature provided for that purpose, we found a launch that someone had pulled onto the sand.

Rowboats are another rare thing on the island, as the ocean currents made them unsafe except in the protected harbor at Worldview; certainly few people would have been mad enough to try to use one to cross the reach to the mainland. But they could sometimes be trusted by travelers circumnavigating the island, as long as they stuck close to the shore and weren't mad enough to make the attempt in rough weather. This boat looked ancient and battered, and not like a vessel anybody would have wanted to take to sea. A hand's depth of filthy black water sat in its hull, and of the two distressed oars leaning against its one seat, one was cracked most of the way through, and held together with cords.

We knew most of the island's boats on sight, but this one was too unremarkable to be identified as either one they knew or one they didn't. We regarded it with the concern of Worldview villagers who knew how unlikely it would have been for any stranger to have traveled to this precise spot, with only this insufficient vessel standing between them and the open sea.

Partyka examined the furrow the boat had left upon being dragged from the water. "It's only been here a couple of hours."

I searched the tree-line. "Should we look for whoever it belongs to?"

"If they were able to get here they should be able to get back."

"I suppose. But . . ."

Then we saw movement on an outcropping of rock just south of us.

He emerged from behind a stand of sea stone, a lean and scarred but powerfully-built fellow with gray stubbled hair, a jaw too squared for the lines of his face, and a smile that revealed more teeth on the top than he was able to match on the bottom. Missing front teeth tend to make people look stupid, an unfair fact of life, but there was too much understanding in his eyes for me to make that mistake of him; his mind was working, measuring me and Partyka and reading our impulses as soon as we had them. He was barefoot. He wore a canvas shirt too large for him, the cords that were supposed to be tied across his chest frayed and dangling in a manner that suggested he hadn't bothered to tie them for quite some time. His pants were similarly frayed at the ankles. The clothes had the greasy, transparent look clothing picks up when it hasn't been cleaned, or changed, in a while. They were bright yellow, and as easy to identify to anybody growing up within sight of the prison's lights as the sudden shadow of a predator would be to any little fish trolling the shallows in search of the detritus left by others.

Driven by shock, Partyka said something stupid and obvious. "That's a prison uniform."

"Nothing gets by you," the gap-toothed man said.

We had not heard of any prison breaks on the mainland, where the great iron bells rung when a convict goes missing are loud enough to be heard here so far across the water. We had indeed never heard of any fugitive mad enough to flee not deeper into the interior, despite all the barriers that would stand between him and a successful flight to places where no one might know him. But there was no other reason for the man's dress, for his smile, for the way his cold eyes measured us.

Partyka grabbed me by the wrist and tried to pull me back into the forest. But even as we darted for the trees, three other similarly-clad men emerged from the tree line, trapping us with the harbor at our back. One was a giant, with bulging arms and a gleaming forehead; another, who only came up to his chest, had the slack-jawed, semi-dazed gaze of the simpleton. The fourth was the most scared looking: a boy, not much older than us.

Somehow, I feared the simpleton most. He had the look of a man who smashed skulls and experienced bafflement when red stuff came out. But I headed in his direction, judging him to be the weak point in this four-sided cage. It turned out that if the creator had short-changed him in mind, she had given him compensating gifts in reflexes. He quickly shifted to intercept me, and I had to back off, as did Partyka. The net contracted, my promised and I left back to back, trapped animals surrounded by a closing pack.

"Don't hurt us," I said.

Their leader, the gap-toothed man smiled, showing rotten gums. "Now, why would we do that?"

"Because that's the kind of people you are? Because it suits you?"

"Because we've been months or years without being inside a woman," the boy suggested.

"Save it," snapped the gap-toothed man. "I don't want to use them up until we've had a proper talk."

"Fine with me," the boy said. "I just claim first rights on the girl."

In many of the adventure stories I've read, there's a point where the beautiful girl faints out of terror, thus making her a greater burden to the hero who must risk his neck to rescue her. I've never accepted that, but found to my dismay that it was not as unrealistic a premise as I'd supposed; somehow, our predicament had made breathing difficult, and the black spots gathering at the edges of my visions threatened to swarm together and become the black that comes just before falling to the ground. I gulped air and felt better. "What are you doing here?"

"I could ask that question," the gap-toothed man said.

"We live here," Partyka snarled.

"You live in that little village we were smart enough to avoid. You don't live here, on this side of the rock."

I said, "You've never taken a walk?"

The gap-toothed man was amused by that. "Yes. Recently."

"Why didn't the escape bells toll?"

"If we planned correctly," he said, "nobody knows we're gone. You're looking at four gents who they threw into a dank basement and forgot about. In a week they'll open it up just to see if we're still alive. They'll find the place where we broke through the wall. It's the only place in the prison that could have given us such a splendid head start."

"But why trap yourself *here*?"

"It doesn't take any deep thinking, girl. We were prepared to winter here in privacy, living on fish, and make it back to the world after everybody thought we were safely dead. We were going to be good neighbor and make sure we were out of everybody's way, all that time. We didn't bargain on being spotted on the first afternoon. That was bad luck, island girl; bad luck for us." He showed gums. "And especially bad luck for you."

The four of them moved closer, testing us, really just playing with us, seeing how much they could hem us in before we lashed out or tried to make a break for it. The two of us went back to back, Partyka raising his fists, me folding my hands into claws, both of us aware, as these predators were, that if it came down to a fight it would be a short one, with us dead at the end of it. I thought of all the heroes whose stories I had told, who had lifted sword or dagger or just well-trained arms to battle forces superior in number; and of how many of them had laughed in the face of such dangers, a reaction that now struck me as imbecilic.

Partyka said, "We won't tell anyone."

The gap-toothed man said, "I have no problem believing that you think that, boy. I believe you'll head back to the village you came from and that you'll keep the promise for a few hours, until it occurs to you to worry about the danger we represent to any other idiot children who might wander to this part of your little rock we've claimed for ourselves. I think you'll spill by morning, either blood or words. So for our sake it might as well as be blood."

The giant and the simpleton drew closer even as their leader spoke. There were still empty places between the four of them, of course, but just to dart through any of the available gaps was to tempt the moment when they leaped to intercept us, a chance that grew more and more slim the closer they came.

But even that wasn't the biggest danger. I could feel the muscles of Partyka's back, pressed against mine as we tried to present these villains with a united front, bunched up as he transparently did what boys do and calculated the most effective place to throw his first punch, the best sequence of fight moves to prove himself a hero capable of defending me—all of which I appreciated and even loved, but knew to be as wrong as wrong can be. Partyka was slight. He wouldn't prevail in a fight against even one of them.

It was less to stop the advancing men than to stop Partyka from getting himself killed that I said, "Don't be stupid. We're your only hope."

• • • •

This was a fresh development, one that the gap-toothed man was not stupid enough to believe right away. The skepticism showed on his face, complacent and superior and utterly experienced in the kind of desperate things a frightened person might say, when faced by a beating or worse. But I think he was disturbed by the way I had said it, with urgency not at all diluted by fear; with no tremor, but only scorn.

He raised his hand, halting the others. "Really, now."

"You have the time to hear me out," I said. "Look at us. You've got us trapped."

"Yes. And so you have nothing left but words."

"True. But nobody's watching. Nobody's running to get help. I can take my time telling you what you have to know, and you'll still have the option of having your fun with us, afterwards. It's my guess that by the time I'm done you'll see it's the stupidest possible thing you can do."

"We weren't planning on asking your advice," said the boy.

I curled my lip. "That's because you don't know well enough to consider it."

A storm passed over the boy's face, so dark that I feared him lunging to strike me. That would come, sooner or later. He was an angry one, as I supposed one would have to be to wind up in a prison while barely old enough to shave. If an attack came, it would come from him.

"This is just playing for time," the gap-toothed man said.

"Of course it is. I want to live. I want Partyka, here, to live. But I only have one thing to bargain with and that's what I know. You can tell me if what I have tell you is worth it."

He flashed a grin in what almost qualified as affection. "Very well. Clock's ticking."

"All right," I said. I glanced over my shoulder and made eye contact with Partyka, whose expression reflected a terror that was only slightly abated by this strange twist events had taken, before it burst forth as panic. I saw his mind working, trying to fit the pieces together, finding no place where they melded to form a picture. Then I nodded and did the last thing anybody around us expected. I sat, and with a tug on his wrist, pulled him down beside me.

"You might as well get comfortable too," I told the others.

The simpleton sat without further bidding, stunning the giant. The young one glanced at the gap-toothed one, awaiting instructions; that he apparently received, because he lowered himself into a crouch of the sort that would kept him free to leap to his feet in a heartbeat. The giant, receiving different unspoken instructions, remained standing; as did the gap-toothed man himself, who folded his arms over his chest, with a patience that was already waning.

I said, "First question before we start, so I know the stakes here. You're all murderers, right?"

The gap-toothed man nodded. "Among other things. I've done four. The big one's done five. All in the course of business disputes. We were tradesmen, I suppose. The idiot and his excitable young friend are more passionate types: brothers who teamed up to do one between them, a girl your age who was better off dead when they were done with her. But there isn't a one of us who would hesitate to put down a stupid boy and a chatty girl, if it put off our return to that place by so much as one day. You're lucky enough we'll let you live a while first, for entertainment. The kid's been fretting. And your clock's still ticking. Get on with it."

I did the hardest thing I've ever done, and smiled at him, hoping he hadn't heard the wet gurgle at the base of my throat. "Understood. Just figuring out where we stand.

"So here, just to start, is why you *have to* listen to me.

"If this meeting between us was happening anywhere inland, you would have options. You would just kill us, get rid of the bodies, and run. Those who loved us would have to search all four points of the compass, and if they didn't find us, would never know if they'd searched hard enough. If we were a boy and girl near a big city where we were two of many, our absence might not even be a big deal, for a while; there are just too many places we could have gone, on even a typical day, for anybody to think anything other than we were just running away or just late getting back home.

"But this is an island, where *everybody* knows us. Kill us and we'll be missed in hours. Kill us and by *nightfall* you'll have two hundred worried people with lanterns, scouring every grain of sand on this island. You'll won't be making yourself any safer. You'll just be guaranteeing that you get caught that much faster."

He rubbed his chin. "We could make it look like you got killed in an accidental fall. We'd hide until you were found, and not come back out until your loving families dragged you back home for the funeral."

"You could," I said, without any special heat. "If the island wasn't shaped it the way it is, it might even work. But pretty much all the high places around here are on the side facing the water, and that means that if we fell we'd be carried out to sea. If we fell from a high place we would never be found."

"That's a fine argument in favor of us drowning you."

"Not at all," I said, "because it leaves you with the same problem. Even if we vanished off the face of the Earth tomorrow, even if our families were left thinking we went to one of the cliffs and leaped off, in some foolish lover's quarrel, they still wouldn't give up on us until they knew that was the only possibility. You would still have that search party setting out from the village and examining every inch of every trail before they gave up. They'd even get dogs from the mainland.

"You can't stay ahead of a search like that, not on an *island*.

"And it gets worse after a few days. If we go missing, word will get back to the continent within a day. Sooner or later, your jailers will realize you're gone, too. They'll do the basic arithmetic and wonder if you didn't head across the water. They'll send more, meaner people to join the search for us, trackers with ways of following a trail not known to people who fish for a living. They'll find signs of you and they'll drag you back to your cells, if they don't see fit to kill you first.

"I'm telling you, mister, you can't *afford* for anything to happen to us. You need us alive, well, and accounted for. That's not the thing I have to tell you, just why it's important."

The simpleton wasn't following any of this, but the kid and giant were; and so, most importantly, was the gap-toothed man, turning grimmer and more desperate as all his hopes of freedom fell to pieces before him. I glanced at Partyka, who was not much happier; he had no idea where I was going with this.

"Your clock's still ticking," the gap-toothed man said.

I said, "You know where you are: the only inhabited island in the entire ocean."

"The only island," he said.

"The only *inhabited* island."

"The only *island*," he repeated.

"Use some sense. You think it's really just deep water, everywhere? You think the same god that put islands in rivers and lakes didn't pepper the world with outcroppings of land wherever the sea water is shallowest? Of course he did. There are other specks of land, here and there, some of them just a few hands across, some of them just big enough to stand on long enough to decide that you were better off in your boat. There just aren't any that are both big enough, and close enough to land, to be worth the trouble of settling. The one we're on right now, this little piece of nothing, is pretty much it. You could get in that boat and travel all the way around the world and not find another island big enough to support two hundred people.

"But that doesn't mean there isn't one, within reach, that can support *four*."

* * * *

For a few seconds the only sound in that little inlet was the soft splash of some little wavelet, whispering against the sand, and distant sea birds, keeping each other informed on the locations of all the best fish.

There was also Partyka's hand, shifting against the sand at my thigh: a small, random movement, impossible to mark as anything but a body's natural desire to move whenever it has been at rest for too long. The action left his fingers buried in dirt to their midpoints, a means of clutching sand he could hurl in someone's eyes. I glanced at him to make sure that his own reaction to what I'd said wouldn't give us away, and was rewarded by a persuasive, sinking look of resignation: like he couldn't believe that I'd traded away such a valuable secret, without receiving any assurances in return.

The boy said, "She's lying."

He was coiled, like a dog seeking the softest place in an opposing dog's throat. He was excited, too; happy about it, grinning over the prospect of having a girl to play with. The gap-toothed man would have killed us out of convenience, the giant and the idiot because they would see no reason not to. That little animal would kill us for fun.

So I smiled at him. "Am I?"

The hand of the gap-toothed man had gone back to rubbing his chin. "They've always called this the only island in the sea."

"They also talk of the four corners of the Earth," I replied, with irritation, "and you do know it's round, right? Or are you too *stupid* and *ignorant* to know that?"

"Watch yourself, girl."

"Why should I? I'm not about to get in any worse trouble." But then I realized that I might have gone a bit too far, and spoke quickly: "Think about it. They call this the only island because it's the only one that's useful to people. But I've *been* to another, a smaller one, a *not useful* one, two hours of hard rowing to the east. I took my father's boat there, just to show I could, when I was nine. I got in trouble for doing it, but I did it. Are you actually telling me that you can't row as hard as a nine-year-old girl?"

"Keep talking," the boy said. "I'll wipe that grin off your face."

"In the creator's name, I've already shown you that you *have to* let us go if you have any sense, what reason would I have to lie after that? Listen to me. The island you need to get to is called Crab Shoal. In the old days, when explorers went out to look for more land worth having, they found it, looked it over, decided that it was the most pointless rock that ever existed and drew circles around it on their maps, just to make sure no stupid fisherman ever bumped into it by accident. Then when they decided that since there was no reason for anybody to go out that far, anyway, it could at least be a landmark for fishermen, that if they saw it they'd gone far enough. It's just a place that reminds people to turn back, now; a place where sea birds nest, when they're not out dipping their beaks for fish.

"It stands about forty hands out of the water, which is good because you can see it from a distance. It's so small that if you were to put houses like the ones in my village on it, you'd only have room for two or three.

And though it's all black rock underneath, it's blinding white from bird droppings; I'm not saying you could call it luxurious.

"But it should interest you for two reasons.

"First," I raised a finger, "there's a little shallow pool near the water that always fills up whenever there's a high tide. The tide goes out and the water remains. Crabs get trapped. The one time I was there I saw six of them, just sitting there under the water. It's like meal delivery, twice a day. You could pick up enough, in five minutes of effort, to feed the lot of you. That's why they call it Crab Shoal in the first place. Go there and you'll get sick of crab, and fish, and any birds you could catch, but you won't starve, and it'll get you through the winter. There's also rain every couple of days, so you'll get fresh water as well.

"Second, on the eastern side of the island, about two-thirds of the way to the highest point, you'll find a hollowed-out place where the waves have carved out the entrance to a cave. Climb up a little bit when you get inside and you'll find yourself a nice shelter, above the surf. It's never warm, but it's also never freezing. You should be able to hide your boat in there with you and stay there until spring comes and they've forgotten all about you."

"I don't believe you either," said the giant.

His voice was the rumble some very large men have, impossibly deep and impossibly thick, the words mushy and distorted by whatever his gigantism had done to his voice box. It was the rumble that death itself must have, when it knocks on your door in the middle of the night, saying, *I know you're at rest, but I'm here for you.* I could only be glad I was kneeling, because if I'd been standing my knees might have buckled at the very sound. What he would do, with those hands, if it suited him; how much it would hurt . . .

But I gave him a look that would freeze an open flame. "People have done it, more than once. Fishermen whose boats foundered. Folks who couldn't swim back here, but could get to Crab Shoal. There was one man, Ferezin something . . ."

I turned to Partyka to supply the name, spinning my hand for prompt.

Light entered his eyes. "Ferezin Hamper. Melodi Hamper's grandfather."

"Great-grandfather," I said. "Sixty years ago. Everybody thought he drowned. His family held a funeral for him. But he made it to the shoal and survived there for two whole winters before being able to flag a passing boat."

"It was three winters," Partyka said.

"Really only two," I argued. "He got stranded with only a bit of the first one left to go."

"People say it was three winters," said Partyka. "There's a song, I think."

"*My Castle In the Sea*," I said, nodding. "*Where I slept for winters three.* But they made it *three* because it rhymed with *sea*. It was really only *two*."

I faced the gap-toothed man. "So that's what you do. You head for Crab Shoal. You make your camp inside the cave. You spend the winter there. You wait for everybody to figure you've drowned or outrun them. When spring comes you wait for the first clear day and head south when the tide shifts. In about two hours or so you'll pick up a current that will help you make it to rest of the way back to the mainland. You should hit the wooded land on the cape. After that it's up to you."

The four of them stared at us, and each other, with a reluctance to believe coupled with an eagerness to believe that was heartbreaking in the overwhelming conflict between them. I braced my palm against the sand and got back up, stretching. Partyka did the same, except for the stretching part. The kid rose with us, wary in case we intended to attempt a break; only the simpleton remained seated, too slow to figure out that story time was over.

It all fell to the gap-toothed man, who went back to rubbing his chin, as he seemed to always do at moments of vital concentration. "Crab Island," he repeated.

"Crab *Shoal*," I said.

"Yes, that's what you said. I thought it wise to check your memory. And that man who was stranded there was—his name again?"

"Ferezin Hamper," Partyka said.

"Great-grandfather of one Melodi Hamper. *A castle in the sea, where he*—"

"—*slept for winters three*. Yes."

"Do you intend to give us any directions other than *east of here*?"

"That depends," I said. "Do we live?"

"Well," he said, and here his disfigured smile became a crooked thing, "if you can explain why we shouldn't kill you and *then* go. Because no search of this island will find us on *that* one."

"Because everything I said about the search of this island still applies. Sooner or later the people searching for you will realize they can't account for a boat. They might even find signs that you landed here. After that, the only logical place for them to look is Crab Shoal. And even if you think you can evade a search here, you can't be dumb enough to think you'll evade one *there*. It's way too tiny."

"And if we let you go," he asked, "what stops you from telling someone about us as soon as you get home?"

I adopted a baby voice. "*Mommy, Mommy. We helped the murderers escape.* We live within sight of a prison. Don't you think we made rules for each other, about what we should do if we ever ran across an escapee? Rule number one is, *don't help them. Not even if it means your own life. You help them, you become as bad as them.* We tell anybody we did, we'd be disowned by our families and driven from our homes. That's the last thing we want. Better to just be rid of you, cover up any signs you were ever here, and go back to living."

"Fine then. Tell us how to get to this Crab Shoal and we'll decide whether to let you live."

I shook my head. "No. You let us go and I'll tell you then."

"We could beat it out of you."

"You could try," I said. "But what if one of you hits me too hard and I'm no longer *able* to tell you? What if you don't hit me hard enough and I hold on, knowing that it's only staying silent that keeps us alive? Just how much time do you think you'll have to work on us before the search starts? Hours? Don't you need your head start to be better than that?"

The gap-toothed man charged and seized me by the throat. I thought of my mother and father and of everyone else I loved, of the places I'd never go and the experiences I'd never have. Partyka grabbed his wrist and tried to wrench him free, but the man's grip was too strong, his will too iron; it would take a hundred Partykas to loose a hold, from such a man, with such a killing hunger upon him.

Then he released the pressure and cupped my chin in his rough calloused palm, turning my gaze toward his so he could search my eyes at length. I held his look, and allowed a little tremble to escape while he could feel it; even encouraged it by thinking of the kind of things he could do to me, and would do to me, if it occurred to him for even the length of an impulse that it was what he wanted. Nobody had ever read me so intimately, not even Partyka.

After a moment he released me, gave Partyka a look not nearly as penetrating, and jerked his head to the right.

The boy said, "You must be joking."

"I'm not," the gap-toothed man growled. "Unless you have any better ideas."

"You can't release the only girl we've seen in months!"

"I'm releasing the boy too," said the gap-toothed man, "and that's just as big a sacrifice for me, so shut up and do what you're told, or I'll kill *you*."

We didn't stay any longer than we had to. I took Partyka's hand and stepped away, crossing the invisible line between the simpleton and the giant, moving past the frustrated kid, not turning around until the two of us stood side by side at the tree line.

Then we faced them. By then, the simpleton had gotten to his feet. The gap-toothed man was just arriving at his side. The four of them drew ranks and faced us shoulder by shoulder, still dangerous, still seconds from charging at speeds unknown to us. We were only ten paces apart. It was just barely possible that if they decided to come after us they would be the faster runners. But it was unlikely. Partyka and I were younger than any of them, except for the boy, the only one of the four who would be a real danger to us if it came down to a chase. We were islanders who had been swimming in the tide pools and climbing the mountainous paths for all of our lives. They had been in cells, unable to walk more than ten paces without being forced to turn by a wall. We knew every path, every gully. They did not. They had surrendered the advantage. We had taken it. From this moment on, unless they did everything right, and we did everything wrong, they would have to run a great distance to catch up with us, and every step we took would bring us closer to the safety of home, closer to the places where a cry for help would bring concerned friends and family running.

But we had not won yet.

I said, "The tide turns in an hour. Paddle due east, steering about twenty degrees north to counter the southerly currents. You can't stop rowing, not even to rest, because if you do you'll drift off course. If you get too tired, change positions and let someone else row. As soon as you can't see our island anymore, start following any sea birds you see heading farther out. They're heading to Crab Shoal and will take you straight there. When the sun's going down behind you, you'll see it reflecting off the white rock, in the distance. Near sunset it'll sparkle red. You'll see it from miles off, and if you row hard enough get there by the time dark comes."

"Good luck," said Partyka.

The four of them tensed to jump us, but I silenced them by holding a single finger aloft.

"One other thing—"

And then we bolted, the two of us, me leading him because I'd always been the faster, the shouts of the convicts diminishing behind us, the terror that had been burning in my chest finally freed to express itself in tears. Behind me I heard Partyka charging through the green places as furiously as I was, his gasps filling up the whole world, and either filling an unthreatening silence or drowning out the sound of open pursuit. There was no way of knowing.

It was only when we knew we had run far enough that I fell to my knees and he hit the dirt beside his, his arms holding tight as I released the sobs. He kissed the tears away, and I realized something that I hadn't, during the entire encounter in the inlet: that for all that time I'd been more scared for him than I'd been for myself. Imagine that.

We remained in hiding until we could be sure that we were the only creatures moving behind the tree line.

Afterward, by mutual unspoken consent, we took a roundabout route to one of the high places. The sun was setting by then and the sea was a thousand points of fire. It seemed empty until Partyka, whose eyes had always been sharper than mine, spotted a black speck that could have been a piece of driftwood or four desperate men in a rowboat, spending their precious strength on a frantic push in the direction of nothing at all.

My tremor had nothing to do with the wind.

Partyka slipped his arm around my waist. "I never knew that stories could be so dangerous."

I shuddered, watching the speck as it disappeared, aware that the two of us would carry this secret to our graves. "Stories have been known to defeat armies."

THE ADVENTURE OF THE GARRULOUS CODGER

It was in the late autumn of 18—, while recuperating in London from wounds suffered during one of Her Majesty's campaigns, that I received a most remarkable summons from an old University friend of mine. The letter, written in a clean white ink that stood in sharp contrast with the imposing black cardstock that bore it, first inquired over the health of several of our contemporaries, then invited me to tea at his gentleman's club one fortnight hence. The card did not name the club, but it did advise me that our happy past association in the halls of academe had led my onetime classmate to propose me for membership. I was further advised that the precise nature of the society was a closely-guarded secret, that I was not to discuss the appointment with anyone, and that ample transportation would be provided as long as I proved amenable to those conditions.

Intrigued, I forwarded my assent, and arranged to be home at the pre-appointed hour, when a coachman and carriage did indeed arrive at my front gate to provide a ride to the mysterious rendezvous. I confess to feeling a moment of trepidation when the coachman provided a ribbon of black silk and instructed me to tie my own blindfold, but the memory of the no doubt far greater dangers I had survived in the campaign just past swiftly bolstered my resolve. I donned the blindfold and rode in comfort to the appointed place, my mind a cauldron of wild surmise.

After a journey of approximately half-an-hour through what I adjudged to be city streets the coachman stopped his carriage and escorted my still-blindfolded self up a set of stairs and into what seemed to be a large hall populated by echoes. From there he further escorted me into another chamber redolent with the welcome scents of fine brandy and finer tobacco, where he lowered me into a comfortable easy chair and then took his leave. I heard a heavy door closing, and I felt the one-time soldier's unmistakable certainty of regard from unseen eyes.

Then I heard my old friend's voice. "Welcome to the Adventurer's Club, old friend. You may remove your blindfold."

I complied, and found myself in an opulently appointed library, four stories tall, and occupied entirely by men of substance, who were exploring the stacks of leather-bound volumes that rose from ground-level to the ornate grillwork of the skylight high above us. I recognized a prominent architect, two members of the royal family, several high-ranking government ministers, and a number of retired military men known to me by their solid reputations for forthrightness and courage. I particularly noted one odd-looking old fellow in a club chair, who wheezed softly as he stared into the flames that danced in the establishment's one gargantuan fireplace; he had ruddy skin the color of a dried blister and tremendous white eyebrows that completely obscured the shade and the intent of the orbs that hid beneath them. He was undeniably ancient, and no doubt clinging to this life by only the most heroic effort of personal will, but there was also an undeniable sense of history about him, as if the years he had lived and the sights he had seen still followed close behind him, wherever he chose to walk.

"That is the Colonel," said my friend from University. He was seated in the chair opposite mine, and he regarded me with frank amusement as he swirled a brandy in one gloved hand. "You will come to meet him soon enough. He is a most remarkable fellow, who has traveled to all four corners of the globe, experiencing wonders and terrors of a magnitude few white men can even imagine. It is good to see you, Richard."

I returned the sentiments with equal acknowledgement of how deeply this reunion had stirred my heart with memories of our shared misbegotten youth, and accepted the offer of a brandy and cigar as my friend explained the nature of this most curious establishment.

It seemed that the Adventurer's Club was a society composed entirely of the Empire's most remarkable gentlemen: stalwarts all, who had distinguished themselves with their bravery and their spirit when tested by extraordinary circumstances in exotic lands. My University friend had been a member for years, since an incident involving a Leopard Cult in the deepest jungles of the Amazon; I was being invited to join not because of my service to Her Majesty's Government in the campaign recently fought, but because of a far more obscure incident involving an unearthly creature imprisoned in a Malaysian temple.

"Men who have known such wonder and terror," my University friend said, "who have successfully wrestled with the tides of destiny, exist on a higher plane than the common man, and require the fellowship of others of the same high quality. You may accept our invitation, if you choose; or you may leave here, blindfolded as you were when you arrived, with the assurance that you will never be able to find independent confirmation that this place exists."

It was naturally pre-ordained that I embrace the singular honor my University Friend had offered me, and that I start to cultivate the habit of taking the occasional evening in the company of other intrepid fellows like myself. It was an oddly paradoxical form of pleasure, however, in that it featured none of the extreme acts of derring-do that the members had needed to perform in order to qualify for their membership. The library of the Adventurer's Club was a sedate place, a gentleman's place, a sanctuary from the dangers that marked our existences outside of these hallowed walls; it was rare indeed that we even discussed our past histories, preferring instead to spend our long evenings here engaged in the pursuits of fine food, fine drink, and fine conversation. I confess that I was as prone to falling asleep in my chair as I was to examining the many rare volumes that our society possessed in such abundance.

However, throughout the Winter of that year, and the Spring of the next, as I came to know my fellow club members and treasure my evenings spent in their company, I took particular notice of the imposing old fellow my University friend had introduced as the Colonel. I saw that he rarely spoke to any of his peers, that he watched the fireplace obsessively as if in the belief that it provided a window to the days and nights of his past, and that on those occasions when he succumbed to sleep he murmured constantly, and with increasing agitation, as his dreams came vividly back to haunt him. Sometimes he awoke with a cry, drenched with perspiration. From time to time I glanced at him and found myself perturbed to discover that he was intently studying me, in the manner of any old man who finds it necessary to find a younger man's measure. Always he looked away, not yet ready to speak the thoughts that roiled in his breast.

This changed in April of that year, on an unseasonably cold spring night beset by a torrential and thunderous downpour that had those of us in attendance grateful to be off streets that were more like rivers. Smythe had outdone himself that evening, in constructing the fire that warmed the room in the one manner our mutual respect for one another could not, and as we lounged about in the most torpid languor, enjoying its warmth and glow, we turned to conversation of the distant lands we had known, and the spectacular extremes of weather we had experienced. One fellow opined that no country had rain beastlier than India's; another said that he had seen creation turned inside-out while stationed in the Caribbean; another was just beginning to speak of a blizzard in Tibet, when the usually silent figure by the fireplace rumbled, clutched his walking stick, and said: "I once saw a single raindrop that saved Mankind from total annihilation."

Our entire party was rendered instantly silent by the force of this pronouncement.

"You heard me," the Colonel said. "Of all the hurricanes, gales, monsoons, and torrents that have afflicted our race since the great Flood, none was more fateful than the one I witnessed, and none had the historical impact of the single drop of water that started it all." The Colonel turned around in his seat and began to speak, slowly at first, but with a steadily increasing power.

It was the winter of 18— (he said), in the province of P—, an uncharted little backwater primarily known for the poverty of its natives and the dullness of its architecture. I had been sent there following the unpleasant political ramifications of my adventure involving the Sultan's Daughter and the Eye of the Octopus, in the belief that the isolated, backward nature of the region would be able to throw off the assassins the late vizier had ordered sent against me. This would, of course, turn out to be a false assumption, with tragic results for everybody involved, but neither I nor my faithful aide Hennessy were aware of that unfortunate fact yet, and were happily looking forward to what we fully expected to be a simple investigation into the matter of a band of thieves who were then preying on travelers desperate enough to risk the high mountain passes. It was our assignment to shut down those blighters, and in so doing once again free those roads for civilized men. We had no way of knowing that the danger which awaited us on those windswept peaks was far greater that a simple band of heavily-armed brigands, that our paths would soon cross that of a beautiful and courageous young lady with a tragic secret, and that before the tragic and bloody business was done Hennessy and I would experience a night of darkest and most sinister evil that ever—

"Excuse me," said my University friend, in a sharp and commanding tone that belied the seeming politeness behind his words.

The Colonel paused in mid-sentence, his magnificent eyebrows arching slightly. "Eh?"

"We're not interested."

The Colonel seemed most distressed by this. His chin trembled, and his hands clutched harder at his wolf's-head walking stick. "B-but the temple . . . the magic stones . . . the fateful raindrop . . . dear, lost Araputha . . ."

"We are having a conversation here," my friend said. "We are discussing the weather, and we're having a perfectly fine time doing just that, and we certainly didn't invite you to come over here, without being asked, to monopolize the conversation with another one of your shaggy dog stories."

"But—"

"Oh, we're certain that it's filled with heroism, hairsbreadth escapes, a climax which explains what you said about the raindrop, and a final ironic observation capable of wrapping the whole thing in a nice pretty bow, and it's possible that if you wrote the whole bloody thing down and put it in a book you'd be able to find any number of people willing to read it, but you'll forgive my honesty if I tell you right now that the lot of us have better things to do than sit here and listen to you drone on for hours just because you were able to seize on something one of us said as an opportunity to produce a self-aggrandizing segue. We do not have the time, we do not have the inclination, and we do not have the patience. We do not care. Is that clear?"

The Colonel's chin was quivering. He turned toward me, and for a moment I saw straight into his keen and noble soul. I saw that he had lived moments like this an uncounted number of times throughout the years of his association with this club, and that he had devoted all those months to taking my measure simply because he had been hoping against hope that with my membership he would at long last be provided an audience willing to listen to more than the first paragraph of one of his remarkable and varied narratives. There was an element of pathos to the way his eyes softened, to match the earnestness of his plea: "Perhaps you, young man . . ."

I regarded him forthrightly. "No. Sorry."

The Colonel nodded, with infinite sadness but almost no surprise; he must have had years to grow acquainted with the way his attempts to open his mouth usually went. Then he turned and faced the fireplace again, losing himself in its shifting character as the rest of us returned to our previous banter. He did not speak again that night.

* * * *

I remained an active member of the Adventurer's Club for another three years, enjoying the company and the camaraderie, before circumstances once again forced me forced me overseas. The association remained a pleasant and rewarding one that I still recall with great fondness, even if it was marred by several subsequent incidents involving the Colonel's consistently thwarted attempts to regale us with one of his exotic adventures. It was never the same tale; on various evenings, he tried to tell us about a murder on a passenger ship bound for Singapore, an assassin capable of murdering kings with a single whispered word, and the riddle of the man who could only walk west. However, on each occasion, either my University friend or myself or one of our stout companions managed to rebuff the chap with a few harsh words. We never did get to hear one of the Colonel's stories, and we never did consider that a loss.

When I last saw him he was still in his habitual chair, still facing the fireplace, still monitoring every conversation within earshot for an opportunity to interpose his unwanted narratives. To my knowledge, he sits there still, doomed to the perpetual state of frustration he so evidently deserves.

As for myself, I took my leave of the Club the day I received an urgent summons from an old acquaintance who had discovered his wealthy employer trembling by himself in his study, having been driven stark raving mad by the arrival of a parcel containing a worm of a species previously unknown in the annals of science. What I discovered, upon conducting my inquiries, was so shocking, so potentially disruptive to world peace, that only a massive cover-up on the part of myself and the other investigator assigned to the case prevented the repercussions from wreaking havoc around the globe.

But that, of course, is a story for another time.

SURVEY

"Good afternoon, Steph. I'm sorry for the delay. I had to finish the out-processing on one of the prior subjects and it took a little longer than I expected. Would you like a beverage to make you more comfortable? Some water, juice, soda?"

"No, thank you. I'm good."

"The survey can take an hour or more. Are you sure?"

"I'll take a bottle of water, then."

"That's wise. These surveys can be thirsty work, and our guidelines do require our subjects to complete all the questions before receiving their stipend. If you take a break in the middle and return to complete the rest of the questions, you will surrender half of the one thousand dollars. If you take more than one break, or fail to complete the survey, you surrender the payment in its entirety. This is a nonnegotiable provision. Do you understand?"

"Yes."

"You have also been advised that this is, among other things, an exploration of stress on the human animal and that, accordingly, some of the questions may be personal or upsetting?"

"I suppose that's why you're paying so much."

"Yes. Have you participated in many of these studies during your time on campus?"

"One or two."

"Tell me about one of them."

"It was for the Psych Department. They asked me to watch some old Western on DVD. Bend of the River, starring James Stewart. Afterward, they asked me to take a quiz about the plot, to see how much I retained."

"I'm surprised that a young woman your age even knows who James Stewart was."

"I didn't. Not him or the other guy, Rock Hudson. I think that was probably the first Western I ever saw."

"Was it good?"

"It was okay, I guess. I don't really like old movies."

"You remembered the title and the name of the star."

"I have a good memory."

"And you were paid for this?"

"That's why I did it. They were paying fifty dollars."

"Not much work for a quick fifty."

"No."

"And you even got to see a movie."

"Well, not one I liked much, but still."

"It doesn't seem like that study would have had much of a practical application."

"I wouldn't know. They never did tell me what they hoped to learn."

"I suppose not. We plan to be a little more forthcoming, when we're done. And as you know, we're offering substantially more than fifty dollars, with a chance of payment on an entirely different order of magnitude if you elect to continue with further stages of the study. This is a long-term project that's been running for over thirty years, and we have had more than one student in your financial circumstances stay with us for the entire course of their university educations, some earning so much that they graduated free of debt."

"You're kidding. It can be that much?"

"This study is underwritten by one of the largest fortunes in the United States, with significant contribution from the American taxpayer. I assure you that it can be that much, and that if you do well, it can lead to lucrative employment opportunities upon graduation. But first you have to get through the initial survey."

"I'll get through it. I can use the money!"

"Yes, which is why we circulated the flier among the work-study population. Ah, here's your water. Nice and cold. It's been on ice. Thank you, Jane. Will there be anything else, Steph? Once again, would you like to use the restroom before we begin?"

"No, I'm okay."

"Do you understand that this session will be monitored?"

"Yes."

"Do you also understand that the recording will enter the permanent archives of this project?"

"Yes."

"Do you understand that you are attached to leads measuring your heart rate, your respiration, your blood pressure, and multiple other metabolic indicators, and that this information will be used in this study?"

"Yes."

"Are you all right with that?"

"Sure."

"Please sign here, acknowledging your understanding of these terms."

"There you go."

"All right, then. Let's start the recorder. Survey code 2793MB, subject Stephanie Halpern, preferred name Steph. Age: nineteen. Sophomore, Communication Arts. Steph, will you please say something innocuous, to calibrate your voice level?"

"Umm. Hi. How do I sound?"

"Just fine. Now something with lots of Ps, to make sure we get no mike pops."

"Peter Piper picked a peck of pickled peppers."

"Most people say that. Did you get that, everybody? Ah, it looks like we have a green light and are ready to go."

"Great."

"Steph, do you assert for the record that you have agreed to participate in this survey of your own free will? Say, 'Yes, I do,' if so."

"Yes, I do."

"Do you understand that no payment will be tendered until you answer the final question?"

"Yes, I do."

"Do you also acknowledge agreement that some of these questions may be of a personal or upsetting nature?"

"Yes, I do."

"Steph, the man now entering the room works for our security division. His presence is one of the requirements of this survey. He will not be interfering with us in any way, unless there's trouble."

"What kind of trouble could there be?"

"As we have noted, some of these questions can be upsetting. One or two of your predecessors in this study have succumbed to stress responses and physically assaulted their interlocutors. I do not personally believe that I have anything to fear from you, but the project leaders now require the presence of armed security, to forestall such eventualities. Rest assured that if this does become necessary, he is instructed to restrain you with minimal force. You will, however, sacrifice the promised stipend. Do you acknowledge understanding of the reason for his presence?"

"I'm not sure I like this."

"You can leave, or you can acknowledge understanding of the reason for his presence."

"Umm. Okay. I acknowledge understanding of the reason for his presence."

"Steph, what is your life's greatest ambition?"

"Umm. You mean professionally?"

"That would be a fine place to start."

"I want to work in television."

"Creative or corporate?"

"Creative."

"You want to write? To tell stories?"

"I'm no writer. I just want to be involved in production somewhere."

"Any specific ideas?"

"I'm still figuring that out."

"Excellent. Is it fair to say that your ambitions are at least partially driven by wanting to make a difference in the world?"

". . . That almost sounds like you're mocking me. But yes."

"I'm not mocking you. It's perfectly normal for someone your age to still be exploring her options, to still be forming plans for the future. But this will help us, moving forward."

"Okay."

"Steph, are you a violent person?"

"No."

"Has anybody ever accused you of being a violent person?"

"No."

"Excluding childhood incidents prior to, let us say, age twelve, have you ever struck another human being?"

"Yes."

"How many incidents?"

"Two or three, I guess."

"Describe one."

"A couple of years ago, I went out with a guy who got upset when I told him I wasn't going to sleep with him. I had to slap him to let him know I was serious."

"Did he desist?"

"Yes."

"You were lucky. Any incidents more serious than that?"

"No."

"Did you ever draw blood?"

"No."

"You never had cause to scratch the face of anyone as pushy as that boy?"

"No."

"Forgive me: Is this because no other boys showed you equivalent disrespect, or because you were never again that recalcitrant?"

"That's a disgusting question."

"Do you refuse to answer it?"

"No. There were other guys I had to say no to, and other guys I said yes to, but nobody else I ever had to fight to get them to listen."

"All right, then. We won't ask for the percentages. Are you seeing someone now?"

"Yes."

"Have you ever been angry with him?"

"Yes."

"Did you argue?"

"Yes."

"Was there any name-calling?"

"I called him an asshole."

"Do you still believe him to be asshole?"

"He was definitely being an asshole that day!"

"I don't need to know the details. On a scale of one to ten, with one being absolute calm and ten being totally out-of-control, shrieking rage, how close did you come to slapping him then?"

"I guess a . . . four?"

"Four. Excellent. Steph, is it accurate to say that you have never been part of any military force?"

"Oh, no."

"You mean, no, you have been, or no, you haven't been?"

"I'm sorry. I mean, no, I haven't been."

"Is it therefore accurate to say that you've never had to use lethal force against another human being?"

"Yes. That's accurate."

"Steph, do you consider yourself a pacifist?"

"No."

"Is it accurate to say that you have never done harm of any permanent nature to any human being?"

"Yes."

"What about to animals?"

"What? No, of course not!"

"Do you eat meat?"

"Yes."

"So you do harm to animals, but not actively."

"Yes."

"If you were placed in some extreme survival situation where you had to hunt and butcher some animal or starve, do you think you could do what was necessary?"

"I used to go fishing with my Dad. Does that count?"

"I will take that as a yes. Steph, do you consider yourself a liberal, a conservative, a moderate, or someone who isn't interested in politics?"

"A moderate."

"Do you consider yourself a good person?"

"I try to be."

"An idealist?"

"If that means, do I have ideals, sure."

"Excellent. Now, this is where the questions get a little more complicated."

"All right. Should I be scared?"

"That's up to you. Do you want to continue?"

"I'm okay so far."

"For the next part, you will need your pencil."

"Okay."

"I'm now handing you a graphic on a sheet of paper. Please describe the illustration."

"Three people."

"Can you characterize the drawing, for the record?"

"Characterize it? You mean, describe it?"

"Yes."

"Okay. It's not a realistic drawing, not one that tells me much. It's just three identical black outlines, vaguely shaped like people."

"In short, Steph, is it the kind of drawing you would produce if you had three human beings lie flat on the ground and outlined them with chalk or masking tape?"

"Like they do in murder investigations, right?"

"Yes. Except that we intend these outlines to represent upright, living figures."

"Yes. I can see that."

"Can you tell anything about the individuals illustrated here? Their ages? Their genders? Their racial background? Their politics? Their clothing?"

"No."

"Is it fair to say that they could be anybody?"

"They seem to be adults."

"That's excellent. Children have different bodily proportions. So do some adults, of course—the height-challenged, the deformed, the obese, the disabled, amputees, and so on. I will, however, establish of these outlines that they could very well represent adults of any of these outlying physical constituencies. For the sake of the next exercise, you need only imagine three people living somewhere in the world, their names and circumstances unknown to you. Each one of them could be anybody, from some Mumbai street person to whatever famous musician whose work you enjoy most."

"Okay."

"Is it fair to say that you have no opinion on any of these people? Positive or negative?"

"Yes."

"You are wholly impartial?"

"I can't wait to see where you're going with this."

"Please answer the question. You are wholly impartial?"

"Yes."

"Okay. Now you will play God, for a moment. You will use your pencil to draw a big X over one of these three outlines, in effect killing one of these three unknown individuals. Use whatever imaginary criterion you have. Decide that he's a Nazi war criminal or just an asshole like that boy you once had to slap. Kill him by drawing an X."

"Okay."

"I can see which figure you crossed out, but for the audio record, was it the outline on the left, the outline on the right, or the one in the middle?"

"For the record, it was the one on the right."

"You decided that this individual did not deserve to live and, as a result, some assassin staking out that individual just walked up to them, wherever they are in the world, and put a bullet in their brain."

"Yup."

"Did you feel any sense of satisfaction on killing this person?"

"No."

"Do you feel any guilt?"

"It's just an outline on a sheet of paper."

"Yes, Steph, it is. But this is the point in our session where I advise you that this exercise has never been hypothetical."

"What?"

"I never told you that the three people represented by these figures were imaginary. I told you that they were upright, living people, somewhere in the world. One minute ago, all three of them were living human beings, minding their own daily business. All three of them were under surveillance by representatives of this study, and all three of them were targeted for a bullet in the brain, on your say-so. You elected which one was going to die. Do you see the light that just went green on my console?"

". . . Yes."

"That light confirms that the individual you selected is already dead."

"That's not funny."

"It is not meant to be."

"I get this. This is like, I read about it last semester, what's it called . . . the Milgram Experiment. They coerced people into giving others electric shocks. Except that the buttons they were pressing weren't hooked up to anything. This is like that."

"I'm impressed that you can cite the Milgram Experiment. You're a smart young lady. But this is the precise opposite of the Milgram Experiment. In that case, participants were encouraged to believe that they were doing real harm, when they were not. Here, you were given every reason to assume that your kill order was not real, when your decision actually did represent life-or-death consequences. Rest assured, Steph. You just ordered the death of an actual human being."

"Stop saying that!"

"Please observe the monitor."

"Oh, my God."

"This is a street scene in Yangon, also known as Rangoon, in Myanmar. That unfortunate woman you see bleeding out is one Daw Kham Keow, age thirty-four. You can tell from the damage to her cranium that the firearm used in her execution was powerful enough to ensure her immediate death. You can also tell that our assassin is nowhere in sight. It may interest you to know that your chosen target was a mother and the sole supporter of her four children, all of whom will now become wards of the—"

"Turn it off!"

"As you wish. If you're interested, the two other people you could have chosen to eliminate were one Marlie DeBauer, eighty-seven, a resident of a retirement community in Boca Raton, Florida; and Ga-Heon Teitikai, twenty-four, a resident of Tarawa in the island nation of Kiribati."

"This is bullshit!"

"If you are having any difficulty processing this information, reflect that with the same act you also saved the lives of Marlie and Ga-Heon, both of whom are still breathing only because you directed the fire somewhere else. It can be said that all three were endangered, and that you selflessly saved two of them."

"I'm leaving!"

"That is your right. However, our security officer here has been instructed to keep you in this room until you have been told why you may not want to."

"Fuck you!"

"The two individuals whose lives you spared are hostages to your continued participation. I can promise you that if you terminate the survey at this juncture, the protection you have provided them will be rescinded, and they will also be cooling sacks of meat by the time you make it to the hallway. You will, in case you're wondering, be sent all the relevant photographs and local news coverage, to confirm that this is not hypothetical."

"You son of a bitch! You sick, sadistic—"

"By all means: Get it out."

"—piece of shit—"

"Most people taking this survey respond as you have, at about this point in the process. Some succumb to total hysteria and are unable to continue, regardless of the consequences. It has been our experience that the most principled, the most principled, do regain control of themselves and push on, recognizing that they have no other choice. I advise you to drink some of your water now. It is what it appears to be and is not adulterated with any mood-altering substances. Taking a pause of that nature will help clear your mind for the next phase."

"What makes you think y-you can—"

"The answer to that question is 'experience.' As I told you at the outset, this project has been ongoing for thirty years. It has included thousands of people and involved substantial investments in infrastructure, up to the very highest corridors of power. I believe I can get away with this because everybody involved in this project always has, and it would take a rebellion far beyond your powers or mine to stop it. Now take a drink of water."

"Oh, God."

"Do what I say. It's just water. No unadvertised substances to affect your reactions."

"I don't believe you."

"I have not lied to you yet. Hydrate. Get your breathing under control."

"You son of a bitch."

"Good girl. Listen to me. We know that this has been traumatic. It's possible that, later on, after you leave this facility, you might want to indulge in something alcoholic. In that event, you may use some of your stipend to go on a total bender, as approximately twenty-seven percent of our participants do. It's wholly understandable. Or you may wish to go even harder. If you end up feeling that the rest of your life now offers no options beyond seeking total oblivion, or destroying yourself, then we have ample supplies of crack and meth and a staff of medical experts fully trained to instruct you in the techniques required to surrender the rest of your life to their habitual use. Our people can, if you wish, take you through one safe dose and let you go, or, as some past participants have requested, guide you all the way down to the comforts of rock bottom in one of the facilities we maintain for that purpose. But right now, water will do."

"F-fuck you!"

"You need to internalize this, Steph: I have heard that many times, from any number of clean-cut young men and sweet young women before you. It will do you no good to keep on saying that, because it affects me not at all and does not change your predicament in the slightest. In the meantime, we must either move on to the next phase, or sacrifice the two innocents whose lives you have saved. Should I give the kill orders?"

"No! Don't! I'll cooperate!"

"Marlie and Ga-Heon are accordingly out of danger. See how simple that is? Now we move on to the next part of the survey. For the record, I am now handing you another sheet of paper, bearing graphic representations of five more individuals. Do you acknowledge receipt?"

"Oh, God."

"Failing to answer the question a second time will have the same effect as drawing an X over all the outlines. Do you acknowledge receipt?"

"I . . . acknowledge receipt, fucker."

"Will you please tell me the difference between these five humanoid outlines and the three you were provided before?"

"These . . . look like . . ."

"Trailing off does no good. Please finish the sentence."

"Ch-children."

"That is correct, Steph. In point of fact, these five outlines represent five existing individuals between ages four and fourteen. They may be of any nationality, any race, any gender, any religious background. To make things more interesting, I will tell you that one is an impoverished orphan living in a refugee camp who can hear the pounding drumbeat of war every night from the pallet she shares with four others. Another is the unsuspecting child of a billionaire who believes that the paid companions with whom he shares today's expensive play are friends, and not operatives fully prepared to deliver him to the fate you might select. The three others are individuals of more middling circumstances, though of course of diverse backgrounds; all in all, a handful of lives that would never intersect in any other way, except in this moment when all five sit represented on the sheet before you."

"And I have to d-decide which one's going to die?"

"No. We don't expect you to decree death for a child. Too many test subjects have fallen into complete paralysis at the very prospect."

". . . What, then?"

"You are to select two. One of those two will be blinded with acid, but will otherwise enjoy whatever opportunities are presented by life circumstances. Who knows, it might even be the billionaire's son, who's never going to want for anything, anyway. The other will be taken from home and delivered to a dark, airless room at a black site known to us, there to live as long as medical science can ensure his or her health, but never again allowed the company of another human being, rather to be doomed to an existence where the key question—Why?—will never be answered."

"Oh, God."

"If you select neither, or if you refuse, then all five will be abducted and delivered to sex traffickers. We have a particular dealer in mind. I could provide you with the details of the treatment they will receive under his stewardship, but you don't need to put yourself through that. You just need to know that if you mark two figures with the X, the remaining three will avoid that fate entirely, and that one of your selected two will only suffer a disability with which many millions of people are able to function every single day. The path of lesser evil seems obvious, but again, a certain percentage of subjects who passed this way before you were unable to force themselves to make the selection, and so they chose hell for all five by default."

"I can't do it!"

"That is, as established, a possible outcome. In such a case, you will know for the rest of your life that what happened to all five was your fault. And we will make sure that, wherever you live, however far you attempt to run, you will receive regular photographic updates of how they're faring."

"I'll kill myself first!"

"This will be among your options. Again, once we are done, if that is your desire, we will be happy to provide you with expert assistance as to methods and procedures. But it won't affect what happens to these five. Your only means of saving three (four, really, because blindness is not all that bad compared to the greater threat that's been made) is to provide your marks."

"I f-fucking swear to God, I will k-kill you with my bare hands, someday."

"A genuine possibility, Steph, but one outside the scope of this survey, and one that won't affect this particular decision. You are running out of time. I think I should start the clock. You have thirty seconds to save three by condemning two. Starting now."

"No, wait!"

"Twenty-five. Twenty."

"Why are you doing this?"

"Almost down to ten. Now. Nine. Eight."

"FUCK YOU!"

"The subject is overwrought right now, but for the record, she has drawn the two X's that were required, one on the figure furthest to the left and one on the figure in the center. Her decisions are made. She is two thirds of the way through the survey and has only one section left to complete."

". . . No more. Please."

"I see from the green light on my console that one child has been blinded, and . . . yes—that the other has now been taken into custody and is being delivered to her new life. Would you like to see the video evidence?"

". . . no . . ."

"I promise you, Steph, this next part will the last bit, for today. And because it is the most difficult choice of the bunch, you will be provided with the greatest amount of prior intelligence."

"I don't want to."

"Catatonia is one of your options, Steph. We understand that you might want it and we do have medical means of inducing it. But you might prefer the others I am empowered to offer."

"Please, just let me go. I won't tell anybody."

"Of course you won't. We can dispatch operatives to surveil and, if necessary, eliminate people from all walks of life, all over the globe; you think we can't prevent you from trying to do something about what you know? Please. If it even occurs to you to open your mouth, we'll know it. But you won't. Most people who get as far as you have may suffer emotional problems and suicidal ideation, but they do know the difference between what's feasible and what's not, and don't make matters worse with futile gestures like going to newspapers that nobody reads anyway. They understand that going to the authorities is ridiculous, because we are the authorities—especially if they stick around to ask questions, because they are then told everything they need to know. Let me ask you another version of the same question I posed before. What do you want out of life? Money? Power? Influence? The chance to make a difference? You might qualify for all of that."

"I j-just want to go home."

"You're almost there. You just have this last bit left, and once it's done, you can either return to your life with a thousand dollars in your pocket, or you can join us and be drawn into decisions of even greater import: who lives, who dies, who succeeds, who fails, which economies rise and which ones fall, which injustices are righted and which are allowed to fester until they burst open, laying waste to entire regions with the heat of all that incubated corruption. By the time you're thirty, you can be one of the people pulling the strings behind the scenes, someone richer than you ever dreamed of being, and I can promise that you will no longer feel what you feel now, not anymore. You can—"

"Eat me, you sadistic piece of shit, I just want it over!"

"Do you acknowledge receipt of this last sheet of paper?"

"Yes."

"Please describe for the record what you see there."

"Circles. One, two, three . . . ten circles."

"Steph, those ten circles represent regional populations. Cities, countries. In some cases, hundreds of lives, in others, thousands or even tens of thousands of lives; places that represent entirely different cultures, creeds, and societies. They are residents of democracies, of dictatorships and theocracies, of places prosperous or damned by poverty. Nine of them will continue to bump along the way they have in recent times. The tenth will—"

"I pick one?"

"Yes, and that one will—"

"I've drawn my X."

"I can see that. Do you want to know what's going to happen there?"

"Won't it make the news?"

"Of course. So will a lot of other catastrophic events. Without specific knowledge, you will never know which one was precipitated by your own X."

"Then I don't want to know. I don't want to hear a goddamned thing."

"For the record, then, you've declined all post-verdict follow-up on the specifics of a decision that will negatively affect an entire regional population, out of acknowledgment that there is no way that dwelling on this intelligence could do you any good. Is that an accurate way to summarize your reasoning?"

"Yes, damn it. Yes!"

"That's a wise coping mechanism."

"I don't care what you think."

"No, honestly, Steph—that's precisely the reaction we wish to see by this point in the process. It's been a very successful session."

"Do I get to leave now?"

"With this understanding: that there will be a mandatory exit interview in forty-eight hours. If you have not committed suicide by then, you will be required to return. At that point, we will tell you the results of our evaluation and you will tell us whether your decision-making ability qualifies you for further sessions with this organization, with more decisions of increasing levels of consequence, for accordingly greater levels of remuneration. Before you go, I should mention that as an unadvertised result of this session, you will no longer have to complete course work in any of your classes this semester; we understand that the trauma suffered by many of our subjects does impact academic performance and can therefore guarantee full credit for all classes on your current schedule, at a 4.0 grade point average. If you do decide to continue your association with us—"

"Oh, fuck off. I get it. I get it. I've had all I can take of your goddamned face today."

"What are you going to do?"

"I don't know."

"I can tell you that my superiors will be pleased with how you took control of the last part of the survey. They appreciate that kind of decisiveness."

"They can get fucked, too."

"I feel confident that the opportunities available to you will be significant."

"I don't want to hear that right now."

"Should I arrange the appointment for your follow-up interview?"

"I may jump off a bridge on the way home. I don't even want to live right now."

"Will you promise to wait two days? Hear what's being offered? Learn what other kinds of vital decisions need to be made? What sort of life you can have?"

"That's what's supposed to happen? I'm supposed to willingly give up what remains of my soul now, to join you evil shits?"

"Well, first you have to pick up your thousand dollars on the way out. You earned it."

"Fuck you."

"Two days, Steph."

"Two days."

"Yes."

"To find out what other kind of relentless monster I get to be."

"To be offered further involvement in this project, yes."

"Fuck you."

"And to qualify for substantial employment opportunities upon graduation. Will we be seeing you then?"

"Oh, God. I don't want to be this person. Please don't let me spend my life being this person."

"Steph?"

"Please."

"Steph. We do need to make this appointment."

". . . What time?"

FAREWELL TO FAUST

Posit a man. He could be any man. She could be a woman. They could be any human being anywhere on the spectrum. The story would play out the same. This is, however, entirely the creation of a writer who has written plenty of formidable women, and so he exerts authority for this one time and says that this is a man, who may default to any description the reader chooses, in any home environment the reader pictures. Beyond this, the author takes no position. There is a man, an adult male and in his home environment, facing a stranger who has entered his home and placed a suitcase filled with money on the coffee table.

The man says, "No."

Of the stranger, the reader can make any assumption that rings true. Let us say that he, too, is a man: a prosperous one, formal and polite, with features that default to a mild smile. He has sprung the suitcase open, revealing many arrayed bundles of crisp American hundreds. Put him in a suit, if you wish. Posit him naked as a babe, if you wish, though that is a detail a narrative intent on that image would have to devote considerable effort to justify. Fortunately, the author does not have to. There is the viewpoint character, a man, the intruding stranger, another man; the dynamic precisely and only that: one human being in his place of comfort, the intruder offering an alteration in the status quo.

The stranger says, "I haven't told you what I want yet."

"That's okay. I don't need to know. I refuse."

"You're an odd person."

"I've been told this."

"Nevertheless, you have to be curious."

"Of course I am," the protagonist of this story says. "I'm human. You show me a gift-wrapped present and I wonder what's in it. In restaurants, I glance over at the next table to see what my fellow diners are eating. The desire to know is always a factor. The need to know is a lesser one, one tempered with the knowledge that I'm likely better off not knowing."

"Don't you want me to tell you, at least, how much money this is?"

"I can do the math. Those are bundles of hundreds. They are supposed to be five thousand dollars apiece. Assuming that the interior bills are not, let's say, ones, and that the bundles are stacked in the quantity the space implies, that's about a million dollars."

"It's more than a million dollars."

"Can't be much more."

"It's significantly more. We didn't count out a million. We just filled the briefcase until the grouping was tight and the neat stacks wouldn't bounce around in transit. That's a factor of the interior dimensions, and by the time we were done, the cash totaled one million, one hundred sixty thousand. You benefit from our quartermaster buying a somewhat larger case for this negotiation. Lucky you. It could have been a smaller case, with a smaller sum."

"That's interesting, but my answer is still no."

"May I ask why?"

"Sure."

There is here a notable pause, the visitor waiting for the protagonist to volunteer information, the protagonist waiting for the visitor to give up and just ask already.

". . . why?"

"Because I know the way it works. Nobody comes to somebody's house with a suitcase full of money unless the conditions are illicit, unless they represent a substantial risk to the recipient's life or freedom or unless the conditions of receiving the money are morally repugnant. I choose not to play the game."

"I never said this was a game."

"Everything's a game."

"This money is yours for agreeing to perform a task of our choosing."

"Interesting, but no."

"The terms are that you accept the money first, before the task is specified. If you find it repellent, you may refuse, in which case that option goes away and you are offered an alternative. Refuse that one and you must perform the third, or incur a substantial penalty of our choosing. More options will be presented, with increasing penalties for demurral, until you finally agree to one rather than take the penalties."

"It certainly sounds like a game to me."

"It would. Nevertheless, our key goal here is getting you to accept this money."

"Too bad you're doomed to failure."

There is here another pause. It is punctuated by the sound of a ticking clock, somewhere else in the house. The sound is comforting to the protagonist, an increasing irritant to the visitor.

"You still say no."

"Of course I do."

"You are not in the slightest bit tempted."

"I don't need a million dollars enough to murder somebody for it."

"I never said that murder was a possibility."

"No, you didn't. But it is, isn't it? In the stories it is."

"The tasks are entirely random. Some are value-neutral: like going into the next room and making yourself a grilled cheese sandwich. Or if you don't have cheese or bread handy, going to a local diner and buying one. Others are more unpleasant, like giving yourself a paper cut in the web of your right thumb. These are minor inconveniences in exchange for a briefcase containing one million plus."

"Yes, but the options don't stop there, do they?"

"No. They do not."

"Imagine my surprise."

"The tasks are determined by an algorithm reflecting millions of possible choices. Chances are well over 99% that the first one assigned to you will be benign. If it is unacceptable and you choose to hear an alternative, the odds are virtually astronomical against you receiving another you must refuse; like finding one individual grain of sand in the Gobi against receiving a terrible option on your third try."

"Yes. And having to murder somebody is still on the list, somewhere, right?"

"The point is that of the millions of options available, representing quadrillion-to-one odds against having to do something your conscience would refuse, evil acts are so sparsely represented that there's virtually no shot of you finding yourself irrevocably stuck with one."

"I agree."

"You might be required to spend some Saturday volunteering at a local food bank."

"And that sounds nice enough, but on a philosophical level would be pretty horrible. Me doing something nice like that and getting all the kudos that go along with being a nice person, when I only did it because I've been offered a million dollars."

"The point is that the task picked for you will almost certainly not be evil."

"No. The point is that if your algorithm asks me to do a nice thing, it won't mean I'm a nice person, and if it asks me to do a terrible thing, and I surrender to the necessity, it does make me an evil person."

"But the odds—"

"The odds don't matter. If I agree to play this game—"

"I repeat, I never called it a game."

"If I agree to *participate in this activity*, I am saying that the certainty of receiving a million dollars plus justifies the possibility however remote of being required to do something evil, like kill somebody, or rape somebody, or kick somebody's crutches out from under them. I am saying that the million dollars, *plus*, makes participation in evil an acceptable risk. Even if I say I agree to this and the required task proves to be no more noxious than that grilled-cheese sandwich, I still accept the money knowing that I will still spend my life aware that that having to commit a great crime like murder was a risk I found acceptable. I say no, which is why I've been saying no since the very beginning. I don't need the million dollars, plus, that badly. I prefer to keep what I have."

"You are not a gambler."

"I sure as hell am. I play poker with my friends. I go to the casino, sit at the Blackjack table or press buttons at the slot machine. But the key element of that game, the one that the casino management posts in prominent places to help ameliorate their own responsibility for taking advantage of people with gambling addictions, is that I go with the pocketful of money that I know I can afford to lose. Regardless of what the task I receive turns out to be, I lose much more just by agreeing to participate than I will ever gain by taking whatever that million-plus is supposed to pay me more. You come here and place that briefcase on my table, at the bare minimum you are tempting me in *some* way, and so I am not tempted, and that is why I am saying that from the beginning."

"You've thought this out."

"Never at all before today. I'm just a fast thinker."

"You may not have all the angles figured."

"More than you believe I do. For instance, would I take your offer if you quietly whispered that you're working on a quota and are falling behind on the number of people you needed to entice today? If you quietly showed me a card guaran-*damn*-teeing the algorithm would pick a harmless option for me? If I knew, going in, that all I would have to do in order to grab that million-plus was pluck ten blades of grass from my lawn?"

"I assume that you're about to tell me that you would say no."

"You assume correctly."

"And for god's sake why? You would be guaranteed no culpability for evil acts."

"I would sure as hell not be. You, and whoever funds you, remain in the picture. You are still offering a million-plus at a shot, to total strangers, in exchange for performing an act yet unspecified. Mine might be harmless, and the same might be true for the task provided for whoever comes after me, and for the poor schmuck after that, and the one after that. But the tally is not, *No harm done.* The tally is, inexorably using up the number of harmless results by chance, before someone is finally asked to go after a neighbor kid with a power drill. Even a *guaranteed* positive result still feeds whatever ungodly satisfaction you and your people derive from doing this thing, and that supports the weight you put on the next person down the line, and, again, the one after that. It is only by refusing to participate in any way that I avoid supporting the eventual evil act. And again, only by refusing that I wind up ahead. So, *no thank you.*"

"That's a firm no, then?"

"You're a slow learner. Are we done?"

"No."

"I was afraid of that."

"It is a key element of our business model that in the rare cases where people do say no and won't stir from that position, we assuage their curiosity and tell them what task the algorithm would have chosen."

"I'm not interested."

"Even now?"

"Especially now. You tell me that it was something harmless, like changing the oil in the car, or doing fifty jumping jacks, and I am intended to stare after you in forlorn sadness, thinking about all the money I lost by being a moral prig, unwilling to take a small risk for a large reward. You tell me that it was something horrible, like murdering my next-door neighbor, and I get a jolt to my ego underlying a sneaky belief in my own infallibility. I am not at all interested in the post-mortems. I am much better off thinking that I probably dodged a bullet, and if you don't mind leaving, I'll just—"

"Sorry. We are not yet done."

"It must save you time when some greedy bastard just says yes."

"It does. What would you say if I told you that all this has been a divine test, and that you have passed with flying colors, thus establishing you as one of the ninety-nine truly virtuous people known to exist in all the world?"

"I would say that's pretty nice, and that you can still leave with that ringing in my ears."

"What if I said that only people who pass the test get the briefcase?"

"I would say that's also nice but then repeat that I don't want it."

"Why?"

"Because, even if all that were true, I cannot know it. You have already established yourself as a liar. It doesn't matter whether you're lying for good or evil. You're still lying. The possibility that this is still some kind of manipulation, that you have evil purposes in mind, remains significant. I cannot accept the money with that remaining a possibility."

"What if I provided you absolute proof and left you no doubt?"

"You mean, what if you could *absolutely guarantee, leaving no doubt whatsoever,* that this money was always meant for someone who cleared all your moral hoops and that accepting it would have no calamitous repercussions even by distant association?"

"Yes. And if I also proved to you that the money is yours and that you have responsibility for it?"

"Is this the case?"

"Yes."

Flummoxed for the first time, the protagonist licks his lips and glances at the stacks of pretty, untouched cash. If there is a moment anywhere during this negotiation where he is tempted, it is this one. He is not a wealthy man. He has debts he cannot pay. We establish for the first time that while he has been firm, he has not been unwavering. He could sure as hell use this money. He knows that and now, so do you. He is just confident in one thing: that his integrity matters more.

For a hellish interval, he rationalizes. It is his money, after all. He gets to choose how to spend it. Of course, *taking* it is now a compromise, and possibly a deadly one.

The word *charity* crosses his mind, but it is still self-aggrandizing, still a possible pitfall, and it falls aside and is replaced by the quality that rhymes with it, *clarity.*

And so he says, "Where do you go after you're done with me?"

"To the next person on my list."

"How long is this list?"

"As long as the entire population of human beings. It happens to be true that my associates and I have been bringing this proposition to your kind throughout all known history, but it also happens to be that our own numbers are not infinite and that we do not keep up with your mortality stats. The results we obtain are however statistically significant and stand in for all of you."

"Determining what? Whether the species is damned or allowed to survive?"

"Nothing quite that dramatic. But it does help mold the . . . let us say, allocation of resources toward your well-being."

Our protagonist smiles. It is a nice smile. This is a thing you need to know about this man, who is one specific human being even if in this instant he represents us all. A smile like that can make you think that maybe, just maybe, the world doesn't entirely suck, that things aren't entirely pointless, and that with all the cruelty and nastiness that our kind gets up to, there might still be hope.

And he says, "Then I designate this money to the next . . . player, contestant, candidate, whatever you call us—"

"Participants."

"Yes, that. I designate the money as a strings-free, pre-emptive gift to the next person you tempt with your offer. Tell that person that they get a million if they agree to gamble on evil, and also get it if they decide not to play; the same million, making the choice a fair one. Tell them that if they want, they can also refuse it for themselves and pass it on to the next participant and that if they can keep this going they can help prevent some kind of evil from being committed for as long as possible. Maybe even indefinitely. If they do the right thing, tell them that the guy who went before them gives them a thumbs-up. And that they can pass it on. Is that okay and are we done?"

"We're done," the visitor says.

He stands. He shuts the briefcase with an audible thump, making smaller but still sharp sounds as he engages the clamps. He grasps it by its handle, nods at the man who has refused him, and turns to go—but just before he leaves, he turns back and smiles again. Our protagonist realizes that it is not the polite default smile this man has worn since his arrival, but a broader and more benevolent thing, a gratified and even proud thing.

With this smile, he speaks his final words before departure.

"You don't know her," he says, "but she gives you a thumbs-up."